"YOU MUST NOT COUNT ON EVER GOING HOME AGAIN . . ."

Kirk gripped his cup tightly and waited.

"You see, Captain—may I call you Jim?" Morith asked.

Kirk nodded impatiently.

"Jim. You see, Jim, that storm that *Mauler* encountered was apparently more than just some curious magnetic-ionic disturbance. It was a temporal phenomenon as well," Morith said. His voice, his face, the very stance of his body proclaimed how nervous he was. "*Mauler* was almost destroyed by the storm, but instead, the ship and all aboard her, including you and your Security team . . . well, you were all flung forward one hundred years into the future. That's where you are now."

Look for STAR TREK Fiction from Pocket Books

Star Trek: The Original Series

Final Frontier
Strangers from the Sky
Enterprise
Star Trek IV: TVH
#1 Star Trek: TMP
#2 The Entropy Effect
#3 The Klingon Gambit
#4 The Covenant of the Crown
#5 The Prometheus Design
#6 The Abode of Life
#7 Star Trek II: TWOK
#8 Black Fire
#9 Triangle
#10 Web of the Romulans
#11 Yesterday's Son
#12 Mutiny on the Enterprise
#13 The Wounded Sky
#14 The Trellisane Confrontation
#15 Corona
#16 The Final Reflection
#17 Star Trek III: TSFS
#18 My Enemy, My Ally
#19 The Tears of the Singers
#20 The Vulcan Academy Murders
#21 Uhura's Song
#22 Shadow Lord
#23 Ishmael
#24 Killing Time
#25 Dwellers in the Crucible
#26 Pawns and Symbols
#27 Mindshadow
#28 Crisis on Centaurus
#29 Dreadnought!
#30 Demons
#31 Battlestations!
#32 Chain of Attack
#33 Deep Domain
#34 Dreams of the Raven
#35 The Romulan Way
#36 How Much for Just the Planet?
#37 Bloodthirst
#38 The IDIC Epidemic
#39 Time for Yesterday
#40 Timetrap

Star Trek: The Next Generation

Encounter at Farpoint

STAR TREK®

TIMETRAP

DAVID DVORKIN

POCKET BOOKS

New York London Toronto Sydney Tokyo

This book is a work of fiction. Names, characters, places and incidents are either the product of the author's imagination or are used fictitiously. Any resemblance to actual events or locales or persons, living or dead, is entirely coincidental.

Another *Original* publication of POCKET BOOKS

POCKET BOOKS, a division of Simon & Schuster Inc.
1230 Avenue of the Americas, New York, N.Y. 10020

ISBN: 0-671-64870-5

First Pocket Books printing June 1988

10 9 8 7 6 5 4 3 2 1

Printed in the U.S.A.

To Daniel—
Timely Titlesmith;
Maven of Makebelieve

That which hath been is now;
And that which is to be hath already been . . .

—Ecclesiastes 3:15

TIMETRAP

Chapter One

CAN SHIPS, as well as men, be said to limp?

James Kirk looked around the bridge of the USS *Enterprise*. A less-trained eye would have seen only an experienced group of men and women going about their various duties, competently overseeing the multitude of hardware and software systems that made *Enterprise* more than a mere shell of metals and plastics. But Captain James T. Kirk saw much more.

He saw weariness in the slumped shoulders of his communications officer. He noted the signs of short temper in the abrupt movements and tight-lipped responses of the helmsman.

If a ship can be said to be limp, thought Kirk, *then this one's limping*.

The mission just completed had been more than even a vessel of *Enterprise*'s caliber should be asked to endure. Only the figure bent over the Science Officer's station in disciplined absorption showed no outward signs of fatigue. But then, Spock almost never did. *And yet he was called upon to give more than any of the rest of us, at that outpost colony*. Kirk shook his head slightly in amazement and admiration.

Mistakes would not be made by this crew, Kirk

knew, in spite of their exhaustion, but he was not the type of commander to drive his people unreasonably. *Thank God we're only hours away from Starbase Seventeen,* he thought. *They can have all the rest and recreation they need there.*

I wonder what's waiting for me there. New orders, of course. The ship would be repaired and resupplied, the crew given its chance to rest up, and then both would be called upon yet again to do the Federation's work. Sensitive work, Kirk supposed. Work requiring the best, requiring men and women of competence and subtlety, and a commander who had proven his ability to cope with complex and dangerous situations often enough.

It wore on him, this work. Every year, it wore on him more, and yet he could not imagine doing anything else with his life. For a time, of course, he had had to do something else: a desk job. But James Kirk was not a man who belonged behind a desk. He was a ship's commander whose place was on the bridge of his beloved ship.

But there must be a limit somewhere, sometime. That was his abiding fear. Would someone, somewhere in the Starfleet hierarchy, eventually decide that Kirk was too old for active command, that a desk job was all that he was really suited for now—an aging officer who couldn't even read any more without wearing archaic glasses? Horatio Nelson or John Paul Jones, those two great admirals: which would his own career be likened to? Would he die in glory, at the height of his career, during his moment of greatest triumph, like Nelson, or on land, forced into retirement by intrique and the changing winds of politics, like Jones? A lifetime from now, when perhaps a very different ship bore the gallant old name *Enterprise,* how would history regard James T. Kirk?

Ridiculous, he told himself, suddenly impatient with his own meanderings. *Stop thinking like an old man with one foot in the grave!* "Mr. Sulu," he said aloud, "estimated time to arrival?"

Sulu grinned. "Fourteen hours, thirty-six minutes to Starbase Seventeen R and R, Captain." Kirk could sense his crew perking up at that announcement—which was of course why he'd asked Sulu to make it. It was consideration in such small things, Kirk knew, as much as competence in the big ones that gained a commander his crew's loyalty.

"Captain," Uhura said from the Communications console, "I'm picking up something." She frowned and put her hand to her ear as if holding the communication earpiece would help her pick up the faint signal. "Klingon emergency signal, sir. Heavy interference."

Ginny Crandall, at the Weapons and Defense station, spoke up from Kirk's right. "I have them, sir. Only a couple of million kilometers away."

What're they doing in Federation space? "Let us all hear what they have to say, Uhura. Translated."

"Yes, sir."

From the speakers above the bridge crew came a howl of subspace interference and then a heavy crackling. A voice was speaking behind the noise, but it was drowned out. And then suddenly the interference ceased and the voice barked out at them, heavy and menacing: a Klingon voice, its words translated to English by the *Enterprise* computer but the voice left unchanged.

". . . Klanth, commanding. Failure of vessel structure accelerating. Destruction of *Mauler* imminent. Crew conduct exemplary. Request commendations be sent to clans of all. I personally commend all of us to the gods. Survive and succeed!"

The last words were washed out as the interference returned with a roar. Uhura reduced the volume to a background growling. "I can't get it any clearer, sir."

Kirk nodded, "Spock?"

The Vulcan's face was hidden in the hood of the Science station console. "It appears to be a magnetic-ionic storm of some sort, Captain, and the Klingon ship is in the middle of it. It does bear some resemblance to the storm *Enterprise* encountered in this region some time ago. I'm sure you remember that one, sir."

Kirk grimaced. How could he forget? For hours, he had been trapped in an alternate dimension, victim of a bizarre breakdown in spacetime, the air in his space suit running out, desperately trying to signal his crew during those precious seconds when he found himself halfway returned to his own dimension. In the end, Spock had been able to predict the time and place of the next intersection of the two planes of existence and had retrieved Kirk with no time at all to spare. Another Starfleet vessel, *Defiant,* had been destroyed by the storm.

It had all happened in a region of space claimed by the Tholians, a prickly and uncommunicative people who rejected membership in the Federation even though they were by now surrounded by it. Federation ships had been careful to avoid Tholian space ever since *Enterprise*'s experience. "Mr. Spock, could the Tholians be responsible for what's happening to the Klingon ship?"

"Perhaps, Captain. We know little of Tholian capabilities beyond their ability to generate the web in space with which they trapped *Enterprise*. However, since they *can* generate such a web, this storm would seem to represent a prodigious expenditure of energy to achieve an object they could encompass far more cheaply."

"In other words, no?"

"Probably not, sir. And of course we do know that strange natural phenomena occur in this region." After a pause, Spock added, "The Klingon ship does indeed appear to be breaking up. The structure of the vessel is disintegrating."

That answered the question no one had bothered to voice: Was the Klingon message genuine or a ruse? As if to add confirmation that it was genuine, Crandall said, "Sir their shields are failing rapidly. I think . . ." She fell silent and concentrated on the readings displayed before her. "Yes, their life-support as well."

"Helm, take us in. As close as is safe. Mr. Spock will warn you when we've reached that limit. Shields up. Yellow alert." Kirk could feel the adrenalin level rising, the blood racing in his veins. He could sense his crew responding throughout the ship—responding to his voice, his judgment. As the klaxons rang, Kirk thumbed a toggle switch on the arm of the command seat. "Transporter room. Get the coordinates of that Klingon ship and try to lock on as soon as you can."

"Do you plan a rescue, Captain?" Spock asked. "Regulations do not require that we respond in a situation such as this one."

"This isn't just humanitarianism, Spock. I want to know what they're doing inside our territory. Visual of *Mauler* on screen."

On the great viewscreen at the front of the bridge, an image of the storm grew, with the Klingon ship trapped within it, struggling ineffectually like a fly in a spider's web. The storm was a rough sphere of shifting colors and brightnesses. Parts of it vanished momentarily and then flared out in painful brilliance. *Mauler* was almost totally obscured, but now and then it showed clearly for just an instant. The bridge crew on *Enterprise* could see the Klingon ship wavering, its predatory "wings" beginning to crumble.

The Klingon ship was surrounded by sparkling lights where the storm impinged on its deflector shields, but that sparkling was diminishing even as they watched it. *Mauler*'s shields were failing under the storm's assault.

"Less than ten minutes maximum survival time, Captain," Spock said calmly.

"Transporter room?"

The response came from the speaker in the arm of his chair. "Sorry, sir. We can't punch through the interference. We can't lock onto individual patterns in that soup. We'd have to have feedback from their transporter on the other end, and even then it would be chancy."

Kirk thought for a moment. "Uhura, open a hailing channel." He paused and then spoke in what he hoped was a calm and authoritative voice. "*Mauler*, this is the USS *Enterprise*, Captain James Kirk commanding. We are standing by and are prepared to beam you aboard our vessel. Please lock in your transporter to ours."

For a long moment, there was no reply. Then the voice they had heard before said angrily, "*Mauler*, Klanth commanding. Leave us, Kirk! Leave us to die bravely, like Klingons."

"Bravely or not, Captain," Kirk said soothingly, "you will die without our help. Wouldn't it be better to survive to serve your emperor again?"

"Not with human help!" The heavy Klingon voice was replaced with the rushing sound of subspace static.

"Uhura?"

She shook her head. "Sorry, sir. They're no longer transmitting."

Kirk clenched his fist in frustration. He had to retrieve at least *one* crewman from that ship! Whatever the Klingons' mission, it was something Starfleet would want to know about. "Spock, could one of the shuttles make it?"

"Negative, Captain. The shuttles have far less defense against this storm than the Klingon ship has."

Kirk had known the answer in advance. He had simply hoped that Spock could pull a rabbit out of his hat, as he had done in the past. He found the image an amusing one despite the present situation.

But Spock did not disappoint him. "However, you will remember that we have on board some of Starfleet's new transponders, designed for maintaining subspace radio contact through the severest phenomena Starfleet scientists could anticipate. Perhaps such a transponder could be used to maintain contact through the storm as well."

"Yes, but what good would that do us?"

"The transporter cannot lock onto a Klingon pattern through the storm, Captain, but it could certainly beam one of the transponders from *Enterprise* to the Klingon ship. Then a Klingon holding the transponders could be beamed back to *Enterprise*."

Kirk laughed. "If any of the Klingons would cooperate to that extent. And if they were willing to cooperate, we wouldn't need the transponder in the first place." Something occurred to him. "Spock, what if one man were holding the transponder and another man were touching him. Could they *both* be beamed back?"

Spock was silent for a moment, then said, "I would

say yes, with a probability of point nine nine three. But that's just a preliminary esti—"

"Never mind, Spock. That's only seven chances of failure out of a thousand. Not bad at all. Get one of those transponders to the transporter room immediately. Security, send a squad to the transporter room. I'll meet them there." Kirk jumped to his feet. "Mr. Spock, you have the con." He strode toward the turbo elevator, feeling younger with every step.

Kirk nodded to the transporter operator and braced himself. The *Enterprise* transporter room and the Security squad standing on the transporter platform with him all faded from Kirk's sight. The Security team faded back in again, but the background was no longer the transporter room aboard *Enterprise*.

In its place was the gloomy, cramped bridge of a Klingon warship, underlit and hot by human standards, and filled with shouts and yells and the groaning of tortured metal. Kirk and the Security team were grouped immediately behind the command seat. The seat held a broad-shouldered, powerful figure: Klanth.

Crowded as the arrival of the Federation intruders made the bridge, the Klingons were too preoccupied with trying to save their dying ship to realize immediately who the newcomers were. A Klingon, his eyes on the display of a small computer in his hand, pushed one of Kirk's men aside impatiently as he strode past.

The group from *Enterprise* split in two and moved to either side of the Klingon captain's command seat. But just then one of the Klingons in front of Klanth happened to look up and right at Kirk. He frowned in puzzlement, and then registered what he had seen. He yelled a warning and pointed, and Klanth spun around. He saw Kirk and leaped to his feet.

Moving smoothly and simultaneously, the *Enter-*

prise Security squad surrounded Klanth, gripping his arms and immobilizing him. They also held onto each other and Kirk, forming an unbroken chain, a circle facing outward, impregnable, with Klanth in the middle. Kirk flipped open his communicator, which was slaved to the transponder hanging from his belt, and spoke to his ship. "Transporter room! Mass beam-in. Now!"

On the bridge of *Enterprise*, where Spock sat in the command seat, the message cut through the noise of the storm and filled the air. The forward screen showed the Klingon warship wavering in the grip of the storm. Spock waited for the message from the transporter room that Kirk, his Security team, and the Klingon captain had all been successfully brought in.

What seemed like a vast stretch of time passed, even though Spock knew that it was less than five seconds. If anything had gone wrong, the technicians in the transporter room would be working frantically to remedy it, and his proper course of action was to leave them alone and not interfere and delay them. Yet part of him longed to contact the transporter room and urge haste, or to go there himself, even though it would all be over—Kirk returned successfully or overpowered on *Mauler* and a prisoner of the Klingons—long before he could get there. And so Spock sat in the captain's seat, face and body outwardly relaxed, but his two halves at war behind the calm facade.

And then *Mauler* disappeared.

Behind Spock, someone screamed, a short sound, choked off in the middle. Spock identified the voice as Uhura's. He turned, saw her slumped across her console, and toggled a switch on his chair. "Sickbay to the bridge—urgent," Spock said. "Science station?"

"N-nothing on sensors, sir."

"Thank you, Mr. Hilg. A prompt response." Dispassionately efficient as always, Spock registered the young Ktorran's attention to duty. It was Hilg's first posting—and an initiation by fire.

A signal light blinked on the arm of Spock's chair. He flipped another switch. "Spock here."

The small, tinny voice cried out, "Mr. Spock, this is the transporter room. We've lost the transponder signal! We can't lock onto the Captain or the others again."

"That is because they are no longer there," Spock said quietly.

"The storm, Mr. Spock!" It was Ginny Crandall, at the Defense station.

Spock came back to sudden alertness. In the primary screen, the storm was ballooning outward, filling the view. *Like a living thing*, Spock thought. "Full power to shields, Mr. Crandall."

"Sir," Hilg said, "it's heading right for us."

"Helm," Spock snapped. "Reverse, maximum warp."

But he had been a moment too late. Even before de Broek, the helmsman, could react, the storm engulfed *Enterprise*.

The starfield on the forward viewscreen was gone, replaced by a swirl of glaring colors. The bridge lights dimmed. Everything was bathed in the shifting colors of the storm on the viewscreen. Heavy vibrations boomed through the fabric of the ship. Spock found his entire body shaking, his teeth rattling together; he clenched his jaws and gripped the arms of his chair. Through gritted teeth, he said, "Communications—alert Starbase Seventeen of our position and situation."

"Shields failing, sir!" Crandall said. "Can't bring them back!"

"Helm, reverse, maximum warp," Spock repeated.

"Nothing, sir," de Broek said. "She's not answering."

Suddenly, "down" began to change meaning. Artificial gravity was being disrupted. Crewmembers fell sideways out of their seats. Spock gripped his chair arms all the tighter. Then he freed one hand enough to flip a toggle switch. "Engineering!"

"Engineering, sir!" It was a voice Spock didn't recognize. "Galaym here."

"Where is Mr. Scott?"

"Injured, sir. We're all being thrown"—the sound of a crash—"down here. All the systems are being overloaded by something. We're losing—" The voice disappeared.

"Mr. Galaym," Spock said. "Mr. Galaym!" He toggled the switch a few times, but he knew he'd get no reply.

The lights were fading still further. Someone said, "Life-support failing, sir." Spock didn't bother trying to place the voice, and he ignored the cries of pain from all around him—from the other people around him. He was listening with all of his senses, listening to the ship, to the booming vibrations and the creaks and groans coming from the vessel's fabric. He was listening the way he knew James Kirk would have done. *Enterprise*, James Kirk's ship, was dying.

Suddenly all was as it had been. The storm had vanished; the forward viewscreen showed a calm and empty starfield.

For a moment, Spock listened to the abrupt silence, the absence of ominous sounds from the body of the ship. And then there was a flood of voices coming from the rest of the ship, telling of damage or calling for help. Spock leaned forward and stared into the forward screen. But it didn't matter how intently he stared: the storm had disappeared, and so had *Mauler;* and with the Klingon ship, so had James Kirk.

Chapter Two

AN EERIE GREEN-BLUE GLOW played around the apparatus.

"Nope," Elliot said. "Sorry. Same thing again. Energy leakage. We're just wasting energy. If we can see it, it's no good." He reached for the power switch.

"But, sir!" An agonized cry came from the young woman standing on the other side of the experiment. "I think I'm really close to it! Give me a few more hours, sir. A few more minutes. Please!"

Elliot hesitated, his hand hovering over the switch. Finally, however, he made his decision. "I'm sorry, Brashoff. It was a good idea. Still is, in fact. But you'll need to do a lot more theoretical work on it." He flipped the switch and the glow of escaping energy died away. A faint whine dropped into the audible range—audible to Brashoff; Elliot had been able to hear it all along—and continued to drop in pitch, fading into silence as it did so.

"Great," Brashoff said. "If you don't authorize me to continue modifying the equipment, I'll be transferred, and then I won't have any opportunity even to work on the theory."

Elliot's face stiffened. "I said I was sorry, Brashoff.

I'm not really required to do even that much. Be thankful you've been able to spend even this much time on your pet idea."

Brashoff flushed. "Sorry, sir. I'll go start taking care of the paperwork to wrap this up." She saluted and marched from the room. Elliot stared at her back with a frown, unsure whether her manner indicated anger at his decision or embarrassment at her reaction to it.

From across the room, old Admiral Kim said, "Tsk, tsk. Kids these days. Want everything."

Elliot laughed. Kim always had the ability to make him laugh, even with the most innocuous remark. "It *was* a good idea, though," Elliot said.

"Indeed," Kim said. "Had it been successful, it might have given us a very useful weapon against the Klingons. Still, you sounded encouraging. Once the young woman has developed the theory further . . .?"

Elliot shook his head. He looked around to make sure Brashoff really was gone and then said quietly, "I didn't want to discourage her too much. She has so much promise. But I'm afraid the work was going nowhere; it's a dead end. Getting her off it and onto something else is the best thing I can do for her career. Her idea was a fantasy, really, nothing more."

Admiral Kim sighed. "A pity," she said. "A real pity. Such an *appealing* idea . . .! But of course your judgment is the one that counts. By now, you know, the entire Science Division feels that way about you."

Elliot looked embarrassed. "Everyone places too much confidence in me, I'm afraid."

"Nonsense!" Kim snorted. "Not too much at all!" Obviously sensitive to his embarrassment, however, she changed the subject. "Shouldn't you be leaving abut now? Or have you changed your mind? I don't want to have to order you to take time off!"

Elliot grinned at her. "Since you're twisting my arm, I'll leave right away."

"Where are the two of you going?"

"Luisa wants to go to England." Elliot shrugged to indicate his helplessness.

"England again? Your wife has an unhealthy fascination with the Hole."

"Don't I know it! I've hated that place ever since the disaster. I wasn't there, of course, and now I don't want to go back. It's . . . so changed."

Kim nodded understandingly. "I can imagine how it makes you feel. But you can't talk Luisa out of it?"

"I've never been able to in the past. You know how fascinated she is by England—especially Devon. Anyone would think she had been born there, although in fact she grew up utterly ignorant of the country. I'm the first Englishman she ever met." He paused thoughtfully. "She says my past is buried in the Hole, and she wants to absorb it by being there."

"Ghoulish."

Elliot smiled. "And it's not cheap, either."

"Don't forget your medication."

"No, Mother." A rare thing: he elicited a laugh from Admiral Kim.

He left the room, quite satisfied. Perhaps he did deserve that vacation—for his success with Brashoff.

"But we are already on our way to Starbase Seventeen, Doctor, as I have repeatedly told you," Spock said. "We will be there in less than twenty hours. To be precise—"

"*Don't* be precise, Spock!" McCoy said. "I don't need the third decimal place. What I *do* want to know is why it's going to take so long when I distinctly remember being told by someone that we were only *sixteen* hours away from Starbase Seventeen, and that was a couple of hours *before* the storm."

"Because I am holding us to Warp Factor Two, Doctor. I am not willing to risk greater stress on the ship's systems or structure."

"Spock . . .!" McCoy threw up his hands and turned away from the Vulcan First Officer, breathing in and out deeply. "Spock," he began again, speaking more calmly this time, "I'm understaffed and undersupplied because of what we went through a few days ago, on that outpost. On top of that, one of my nurses and one of my surgeons were injured so badly during the storm that I've had to put them into induced comas while they heal. And in addition to *that,* I have two dozen *other* injured people down here, many of them seriously hurt. It's more than my remaining staff and supplies can take care of. Safely, I mean—safely and for an extended period. The ones with minor injuries, we've already patched up and sent back to their quarters because we were so overloaded. Or sent back on duty in a couple of cases, because you insisted," he said bitterly. "But the two dozen in Sickbay now, I *have* to get to better facilities. Some place without a shortage of manpower or drugs. Like Starbase Seventeen."

"I understand the needs of your department, Doctor," the Vulcan said. He was aware, as always, of the emotional demon Leonard McCoy constantly kept reined in, and Spock wished he could control his voice and choose his words when speaking to the doctor so as to help him in his task. But that was an ability he lacked, based as it was on empathy and understanding of what the other man was experiencing. It was a skill at which James Kirk excelled; indeed, Kirk's facility at that was a large part of his competence as a starship captain. Not for the first time, Spock wished he did have that ability himself.

"However, I must balance the needs of each department against the well-being of the ship itself." Perhaps he could win McCoy's support by spending valuable time giving him a detailed explanation of the ship's status, since he was unable to win that support by playing on the doctor's feelings.

"Our life support and drive control systems were also injured by the storm, Doctor, and if they fail, hundreds of now healthy crewmen will die, not just those you have in Sickbay. I cannot risk overstressing the drive control system or the ship's structure, and because of the storm I do not have enough functioning repair personnel to keep the systems operating should there be a major failure. I have calculated that Warp Factor Two exerts a stress upon the ship's structure and systems that is below the current advisable limits, within a reasonable safety factor, and yet will allow us to reach Starbase Seventeen with an acceptable chance of survival for essential personnel—also within a reasonable safety factor."

"My God," McCoy said slowly, "I've been wrong about you all along. I've always joked about you being green-blooded and thinking like a computer, but I think this is the first time I've realized that you're really and truly devoid of all feelings. It's not the color of your blood that's the problem: it's the temperature. You cold-blooded, unfeeling—"

"As you know quite well, Doctor," Spock interrupted calmly, "my blood temperature is higher than yours. I will expect reports from you every hour on the status of your patients. Summary reports only—totals, not indiviudals. Except for deaths, of course, since I will need to compose individual letters to families."

"Hah! I can just see those letters now! Never mind, Spock. I'll write any letters of condolence myself. I guess with Jim gone and Scotty unconscious, I'm the highest-ranking creature with any feelings on the ship, aren't I?"

Spock chose not to answer and turned to go. Before he could leave Sickbay, McCoy called out, "This isn't the way Jim would do it, you know!"

The Vulcan hesitated and then turned back to the ship's doctor. "On the contrary, Doctor. This is precisely the course of action the captain would have followed. I have arrived at it by logic, and he would no doubt have arrived at it by intuition, but the result would have been the same." He spun about and hurried away before McCoy had a chance to say anything more. He had to remove himself far from the doctor's presence; McCoy's emotionalism was dangerously contagious.

McCoy was not aware, and Spock would never deign to tell him, of the Vulcan's pleas to Starfleet Command to allow him to keep *Enterprise* in the vicinity of *Mauler*'s disappearance so that he could continue to search for James Kirk. To Spock's reminder of the success of a similar search years earlier, when Kirk had disappeared into another dimension in almost the same spot, Starfleet Command had responded with the same argument Spock had just used on McCoy. The argument had ended with an order: bring your ship in and report to the commander of Starbase Seventeen.

Back on the bridge, Spock reassumed the con. "Mr. Sulu, estimated time to arrival?"

Sulu jumped, struck by *déjà vu,* and then answered, "Nineteen hours and ten minutes, Mr. Spock."

Spock remembered that he had intended to ask McCoy specifically about Uhura's condition. She had screamed *before* the storm had struck at *Enterprise,* and it seemed reasonable to Spock that her injury, whatever it was, had happened then, rather than during the storm's attack. But the tense confrontation with the doctor had driven the question about Uhura from Spock's mind. It annoyed Spock that McCoy had had that effect on him: it was annoying and demeaning.

And now he had not heard a question someone had asked him. Truly, conversations with Leonard McCoy had the evil effect of strengthening his human side and weakening his Vulcan. "Please repeat yourself, Mr. Crandall."

"Sir, some of my friends have been telling me about the other time Captain Kirk disappeared near here."

Spock stared at her. Perhaps he lacked James Kirk's empathy, his natural understanding, but he was nonetheless not completely incapable of analyzing human body language or perceiving feelings expressed sufficiently clearly by means of tone of voice. In this case, he could detect Crandall's hostility quite easily. As he became aware of her hostility, he also saw similar signs of disaffection in others on the bridge. Perhaps he would never understand why humans, faced with the same choices as his Vulcan ancestors had faced long ago, still chose a path that allowed their emotions to dominate their actions so completely. "I remember that incident vividly, Mr. Crandall. Did you have a question about it?"

"Yes, sir, I do." She spoke with nervous bravado. "As I understand it, you didn't leave the area. You hung around until Captain Kirk reappeared, and then you rescued him!"

There was no need for her to ask the obvious question. Unspoken, it hung heavily in the emotionally charged air of the bridge: Why are you leaving this time?

"I did not 'hang around', Mr. Crandall," Spock said mildly. "I was able to calculate precisely the moment the two spaces would intersect, and it was that time that I was waiting for. The situation is quite different now. It is also the case that, ever since that time, the Tholians have been extremely sensitive about what they see as intrusions upon their sovereignty. For that reason, Federation ships have been careful to spend as little time as possible in the space the Tholians claim as theirs. Starfleet Command is thus quite correct in ordering us to leave."

"But you could have persuaded them to let you stay, Mr. Spock!"

Overemotional, and they had trouble understanding their own language. "Even if I could have done so, there would have been little point to it, Mr. Crandall. The Tholians are no mean opponents. We still have no idea how they spun their web around *Enterprise*. We do know that we lost a ship, *Defiant*, in much the same way *Mauler* was lost. What would we accomplish by destroying our own ship, as well? Hundreds of us would die, depriving the Federation of our services, and Captain Kirk and the Security team with him would still be lost."

There was no further argument or questioning, but the atmosphere on the bridge did not improve at all during that shift, or the remaining long, slow hours of the trip to Starbase Seventeen.

Chapter Three

FOR A WHILE, James Kirk dreamed he was still in the thick of the fight.

He saw Klanth flinging himself furiously at the encircling wall formed by the *Enterprise* Security squad and almost breaking through. And then he and Klanth and the Security team and the Klingons were all thrown about violently inside the bridge of the booming, groaning ship. He managed to grab the railing around the dais on which the command seat was mounted and hold on, for a moment keeping himself from injury. He had a confused impression of bodies flying past him, of Klingon bellows and human screams. For a moment he floated in zero gravity, holding tightly to the railing, and then he fell heavily to the floor again. The next instant, he was jerked violently to one side, as if "down" were now somewhere off to the side.

Then a sudden feeling of nausea assailed him. But it was something more than the effect of the changing direction of "down" and the resulting abrupt falling and floating, or the effect of the sounds the ship was making as its structure was twisted and flexed in bizarre ways. He felt the nausea throughout his body, in every finger and toe, in his torso and head and arms and legs. And it increased rapidly, almost like a physical force pressing on his entire body. It became heat, a fierce heat filling him. It overwhelmed his mind; he could think of nothing else. All their strength gone, his fingers slipped from the railing, and he was thrown across the bridge. He slammed with shattering force into the twisted, jagged remains of one of the bridge control stations, but by that time he had already lost consciousness.

He awoke slowly.

The noises were gone. So was the nausea. He was lying on his back. He opened his eyes slowly, slightly, but the light was so bright that he squeezed them shut again. Voices murmured around him.

Kirk tried to push himself up, but gentle hands pressed him back down. He had little strength to resist. Slowly, under the pressure of the hands, he sank back down. The surface beneath him was soft and inviting.

"That's better, James Kirk." It was a woman's voice, soft and soothing. "You still need rest to recover."

But there was a faint accent to the voice, and after a moment's hesitation, Kirk recognized it: Klingonese!

Kirk forced his eyes open. They filled with tears, and he could make out nothing more than blurred figures surrounding him. He struggled weakly against the restraining hands, hitting out feebly. They withdrew, and Kirk levered himself to a sitting position. The movement brought terrible dizziness and nausea, but Kirk gripped the sheets beneath him and held on, willing himself not to fall.

"This is not wise, Captain Kirk." It was the same Klingon voice that had spoken before.

Kirk's eyes were slowly growing accustomed to the light. He squeezed them shut, forcing out the tears, and opened them again more slowly. He had been right: he was surrounded by Klingons.

So Klanth had won. Kirk realized immediately what must have happened. Some of the *Enterprise* Security team had been knocked unconscious in the same way he had been, and the Klingons had then been able to overpower the rest and take them prisoner. Somehow, after that, *Mauler* must have been able to escape both *Enterprise* and the storm. Well, he might be weak, but he would fight as well as he could.

His nausea and dizziness were ebbing. The Klingons surrounding him were making no hostile moves but were watching him carefully. In fact, Kirk detected an air of nervousness about them. He was sitting on some sort of bed and wearing a long, one-piece, white covering. He slid his legs over the edge and rested his feet on the floor. He could see winking lights on nearby machines that reminded him of those in the *Enterprise* Sickbay. He knew what that meant: drug-mediated interrogation. "What—" His voice was scratchy and scarcely audible. Kirk cleared his voice. "What have you been doing to me? You can't hold me prisoner. Where are my people?"

The Klingon woman who had spoken before said, "You are not a prisoner, Captain. You are our guest."

Kirk snorted and carefully slid off the bed. He swayed on his feet and would have fallen had one of the Klingons not stepped forward quickly and grasped his arm. Kirk tried to jerk away, but the grip was too strong. Another Klingon, a woman, took his other arm before he could hit out at the man. At the best of times, Klingons were more powerful physically than humans, and right now Kirk was so weak that he could not free himself no matter how hard he tried.

"Kirk! Stop before you hurt yourself!" This was a voice used to command, the voice of a newcomer, an older man who had pushed through the group surrounding Kirk.

Exhausted, Kirk stopped struggling and waited, staring at the newcomer—a Klingon, tall, dark, and saturnine, with a dark goatee and drooping mustache.

"My name is Morith," the Klingon said. "I'm in charge of this base. I headed down here as soon as I was told you were conscious. I apologize for taking so long to get here. Now, get back on that bed. You're in no shape for such exertions."

Shakily, Kirk sat down again. "I don't understand what you're up to, Morith, but I demand that you return all of my people to me and deliver us to Starfleet. I was attempting a rescue of Klanth from his ship when we were captured. It was not an aggressive action."

"Sir," Morith said in a voice that was both sad and gentle, "you are not a prisoner."

"Yeah, I know. I'm a guest."

"A highly honored guest. Look around you, Captain. Does this look like a prison?"

Kirk had to admit that it did not. The room was pleasant and large. Here and there were other beds, all empty. Each bed was surrounded by a wide space, except at the head, where monitoring equipment was mounted. The arrangement confirmed Kirk's earlier impression of a hospital ward, although an unusually roomy and airy one.

This was not at all the cramped, dark interior of a Klingon spaceship. The lights were still a bit too bright for his taste; they should therefore have been intolerable to a Klingon.

The Klingons, though, looked familiar enough. There were seven of them standing around his bed—three men, three women and Morith, who stood directly in front of Kirk and somewhat apart from the rest. Here were the familiar swarthy skins, the black hair and eyes, the heavy, black brows, the strong jaws and cheekbones, the erect, powerful bodies. But looking more carefully at them, Kirk could see that even these Klingons weren't quite what he was used to.

The Klingons he had met previously all projected an underlying sense of menace. But menace was clearly absent from this group. Moreover, they were trying as hard as they could to be friendly; from their behavior thus far toward him, he could almost believe their attempts were genuine. Their faces lacked the animosity he was used to seeing in Klingons.

Military man that he had been for decades, it was their clothing that was the telling blow. It was unlike anything he had seen before on Klingons, and it was quite different from the uniforms Klingons normally wore. The clothes varied in color and form from one Klingon to another. Some wore wraps that looked like togas, while others wore tunics. There was even one wearing a collarless, sleeveless shirt and shorts. The colors ranged from scarlet to plain white; one of the togas was rainbow-striped, the bands of color running diagonally. Kirk felt more shaken by this departure from the norm than he had felt a few minutes earlier because of his physical weakness.

"Well, Captain?" Morith himself wore a simple tunic, Grecian in style, and colored a warm, earth brown. His exposed shoulders, arms, and legs were heavy and powerfully muscled.

"You speak English well."

Morith smiled—a strange sight in itself. Kirk had seen Klingons with fierce grins of cruelty or marital delight, but he had never seen one smile in genuine, relaxed, human-style pleasure. The heavy, dour Klingon face was transformed by warmth and amiability. This did more to convince Kirk that he was not where he had assumed himself to be than anything else he had seen since waking.

"Good," Morith said. "I can see you are at least willing to listen now. I have to tell you something both remarkable and unsettling. More than unsettling, in fact, but I hope to have some other news for you later, when you are physically and mentally ready for it, that will mitigate the shock."

"I'm all ears." Kirk was also not used to Klingons who beat around the bush.

"Later, Captain Kirk. For now, you need much more rest." Morith signaled, one of the other Klingons stepped forward, and quickly—before Kirk could protest or act—touched something to Kirk's arm.

Strength fled Kirk's body and he wilted down onto the bed. He was faintly aware of someone carefully lifting his legs up and placing them onto the bed so that he lay fully on it, and then he dropped into deep sleep.

When Kirk awoke the second time, he was alone in the room. He felt wonderfully refreshed and energetic. He got out of bed and experienced neither dizziness nor nausea.

His uniform lay on a nearby stool, neatly folded: stripping his white hospital gown off quickly, he dressed himself in it. No sooner had he finished than Morith strolled into the room. This time, he wore a tunic of pale blue.

"Welcome back to this world, Captain Kirk," the Klingon said, smiling. Before Kirk could say anything, Morith said quickly, "Yes, this time I'm here to tell you just what is going on. Now you can handle what I have to tell you, whereas before I don't think you could have.

"Come walk with me."

Side by side, the two men walked out of the room and down the corridor beyond. "This constitutes your release from our little hospital," Morith remarked. "We do things very informally out here, not at all like at home on Klinzhai."

Kirk stiffened at the mention of the Klingon home world and then forced himself to relax again. Until that moment, he had been letting himself be lulled into forgetting just who these people were: they were so different from what he had always thought of as Klingons that he had temporarily ceased to think of them as Klingons at all. He had fallen asleep in that frame of mind, and the thought had in a sense become fixed during sleep. Now, try as he might, he couldn't stir up any animosity within himself toward Morith. This man walking beside him was not a Klingon, at least not in the old sense of the implacable, dreaded enemy; this was simply another man, and at that an unusually intelligent and sympathetic one.

They walked in companionable silence for some time. They passed other Klingons, also apparently civilians; these smiled and greeted Kirk and Morith in English of varying degrees of fluency. "Do many of the Klingons on this base speak English?" Kirk asked.

"Most Klingons speak English nowadays," Morith said.

Kirk stared at him in amazement but decided to hold his peace. Morith was obviously having trouble gathering his nerve to say what he had to say, and Kirk felt unwilling to press him.

Finally, Morith led the way into a room containing small tables and, at one end, food-dispensing machines. It could have been a recreation lounge in any Federation starship. *Form follows function,* Kirk told himself. They sat down at a table, and Morith left immediately to visit the dispensing machines. He came back with two steaming cups, handing one to Kirk. "Try it. I'm afraid it's the best imitation we can come up with."

Kirk sipped carefully. It smelled and tasted sufficiently like coffee. "Good," he said. "And now that you've delayed as much as you can . . . ?"

Morith sighed. "I suppose I can't put it off any longer," he said. His voice, his face, the very stance of his body proclaimed how nervous he was. "I've told you that you aren't a prisoner, and that's true. As I said, you're an honored guest. It's also true that you must not count on ever going home again."

Kirk gripped his cup tightly and waited.

"You see, Captain—may I call you Jim?"

Kirk nodded impatiently.

"Jim. You see, Jim, that storm that *Mauler* encountered was apparently more than just some curious magnetic-ionic disturbance. It was a temporal phenomenon as well. *Mauler* was almost destroyed by the storm, but instead, the ship and all aboard her, including you and your Security team . . . well, you were all flung forward one hundred years into the future. That's where you are now."

Chapter Four

KIRK STARED AT MORITH without speaking.

"Jim," Morith said, "I understand what a shock this must be to you—to lose your entire universe, everything you've ever known."

Understand! Kirk thought. *How could you possibly understand?* Nor could Morith see that this was not the first time James Kirk had been marooned in time. Before this, though, he had been lost in the past. Irrationally, it seemed worse this way: instead of imagining the time familiar to him waiting in the future, he had to learn to see it—and all the people who lived in it—as irretrievably dead and gone.

"What about my men? The Security team I brought onto *Mauler* with me?"

Morith shook his head. "They were all too seriously injured during the storm. You must remember how violent that was?"

Kirk nodded. "I remember being thrown all over the bridge of *Mauler*. I managed to hold on to something for a while, though."

"Yes. Presumably, your men didn't manage to do that. Neither did the Klingon crew. Some of your men and some of . . . our people were killed during that turbulence. You'll remember too how physically severe that passage forward through time was?"

"Extreme nausea. I remember that, mostly."

"Exactly. But for a man who was injured more severely than you were, what you experienced only as extreme nausea could be deadly. As far as we can tell from our autopsies, the time passage killed those of your men who weren't killed by the shaking up *Mauler* experienced during the storm."

"Did *Mauler* survive?" Kirk was asking more to gain time, to regain equilibrium, than because he really wanted to know.

Morith nodded. "The ship itself did, although its structure was seriously weakened. Captain Klanth survived, as did a handful of his crew. As for them—"

"I'm in the future," Kirk said softly, more to himself than to Morith. "I'm a hundred years in the future . . ."

"You were severely injured as well," Morith continued hastily, "but thanks to the medical knowledge we possess in our time, we were able to heal you. You may still experience moments of weakness, but our doctors tell me that that should not be a serious matter. They have every confidence that—"

"I don't understand what you are, why you're so different from Klingons I've encountered before." Kirk's voice was filled with desperation, confusion. It was as though he had heard—or absorbed—little that Morith had been saying, as though his earlier intelligent attentiveness had been a facade that was now deserting him.

Morith replied gently, speaking slowly. "A great deal has happened in the last hundred years, Jim. I would say it has been the most eventful period in the entire histories of the Federation and the Klingon

Empire. But I have someone else who will explain all of this to you." He rose, but Kirk grabbed his arm.

"Wait! What do you do with prisoners of war in this century?"

Morith sighed. "No, Jim. We've told you you're a guest, an honored guest. I see we haven't yet convinced you. Have you been treated the way prisoners were treated in your own age?"

"My own age," Kirk muttered. "That's a tough one to get used to. No, you haven't treated me that way. More like a . . . friend."

"Exactly!" Morith said, smiling. "The perfect choice of words. You *are* a friend, and I'll tell you why. Haven't you noticed also how good my English is?" he said with obvious pride.

Kirk grinned. "Better than mine. As good as Mr. Spock's." At the mention of the name, though, Kirk's temporary good humor disappeared: Spock was lost in the past, too, as lost as any of the rest of his crew, or his beloved ship, or the Federation he served. "Yes, I've noticed that."

"There is a reason for that," Morith said. "We—the Federation and the Klingon Empire, that is—are at peace. Klingons serve aboard your starships—and your scientists work in our laboratories. The friendship between our peoples which the Organians long ago predicted has come to pass. I speak English so well because it is the official language of my people's closest and dearest ally."

Kirk shook his head, dazed.

Morith smiled. "Of course you have innumerable questions. You would scarcely be human if you did not. I will try to have all of them answered. First, though, I must point something out to you.

"You, Jim Kirk, are a living artifact from the most

crucial period—incident, rather—in our history. Or in the history of the United Federation of Planets. Therefore you are of inestimable importance to our historians. I understand that you are overwhelmed with grief and loss, but our historians are panting, champing at the bit, frantic to deluge you with questions, and I hope you will be willing to answer at least a few of them. You see, it's more than curiosity. There is a much more vital matter involved, although I want to wait until later to tell you about that."

"You're piquing my curiosity quite skillfully. Why not tell me whatever it is now?" Nothing, Kirk thought, nothing he had known: none of that existed anymore. The Federation still existed, from what Morith had said, but not his people or his ship, and without the ship and the people, what was he? How much of James T. Kirk was there apart from the ship and the people he loved?

"Because," Morith explained, "despite what the doctors may say, I'm not convinced that you are sufficiently recovered to handle too many psychological shocks. I'd like to take it a step at a time, slowly and easily. And I think you need to learn more about this time, the time you now find yourself in, before we overwhelm you with certain facts about the past." Morith signaled to someone behind Kirk.

Kirk twisted around in his chair. One of the Klingon women who had been standing by his bed when he first woke up had entered the rec lounge and seated herself at a nearby table. At Morith's signal, she arose and came to join them.

"This is Kalrind," Morith said. "I've appointed her to be your tutor. It should require no more than a few days for her to educate you as necessary. In fact, it's most important that it take no more than a few days. I have much other work to do, Jim." He rose. "I think you'll find Kalrind more than capable of taking over for me. I'll be speaking to you again in a few days." He walked away quickly.

"So," Kalrind said, seating herself as Morith left, "this is the famous Captain James Kirk. You can't imagine how many Klingon adolescents idolize you."

"That's an incredible concept," Kirk said. He found himself for once embarrassed by open admiration in a young woman's face. This was, after all, a young *Klingon* woman. He supposed Kalrind would be considered attractive by a Klingon. In fact, Kirk could even see her attractiveness, if he made the effort to see her face as a Klingon would. But simultaneously, like a doubly exposed picture, he could see her from a human perspective: heavy-browed, heavy-boned face, strength with an atmosphere of danger. "I'm not sure you realize just how different you are from the Klingons of my time."

"Certainly I know, Captain. I know from three sources. First, there are our own historical records of the old time. Second, there are still many in the Empire who are too much like the Klingons you knew. And third, there are the Klingon survivors from *Mauler*. Klanth and some of his crew."

"Ah, yes. Klanth." How curious that Klanth and his few surviving subordinates were the only other beings here from his own time—the only others, perhaps, who could be expected to really understand how Kirk thought, how he saw such things as politics.

"You see, Captain—"

"Jim. Call me Jim, please."

Kalrind smiled happily, and Kirk had to admit that her smile lit up her Klingon face and made it warm and happy, the same effect that Morith's smile had had upon his face. It was when they smiled, most of all, that Kirk ceased to think of these people as Klingons. But in Kalrind's case, the wide, relaxed smile did more than make her face look friendly: it made her pretty in a fully human sense.

"Jim. That's nice. I've always like your human names more than our own. Well, as I was about to say, it was most of all the change in ourselves that made the *Roj tIn,* the Great Peace, possible. Some of our historians have always contended that the change in our nature was not natural but was caused somehow by the Organians, without our knowledge. The idea is that the Organians became impatient with waiting for their prophecy to come about, and so they decided to force matters along. However, they have always refused to confirm that suspicion, so there's no proof for it. At any rate, after the Tholian Incident, we became much the way we are now, which is to say, very much like you."

"Soft and contemptible, as your ancestors would have said?"

Kalrind laughed. "Yes, exactly. Soft and contemptible. We call ourselves the New Klingons, the *thlIngan chu*."

"Well, I won't try to imitate your pronunciation, so I'll just call you the New Klingons."

"I'd prefer it if you just called me Kalrind."

Kirk laughed uneasily and looked away. He was disturbed to discover that he was finding Kalrind physically attractive—as if exposure was making him less sensitive to the uniquely Klingon aspects of her face. Resolutely, Kirk turned his attention away from Kalrind's physical presence and to her words. "New Klingons. Tholian Incident," he said. "You use these terms without a second thought because you've grown up with them, but I still don't know a thing about them, and I find it all very confusing."

Kalrind nodded. "Of course. I'll try to get to it in a more organized way. I didn't mean to tantalize you with these vague references."

"You're right. I'm already tantalized."

Kalrind grinned and laughed. "By the way, how are you feeling? Physically, I mean?"

Kirk sat back and concentrated on his body, on the way it felt—rather the way it didn't feel, on the absent pain. "Surprisingly good, as a matter of fact. That's strange, though. I remember being thrown about violently on *Mauler*'s bridge during the storm and banging into various bridge fixtures. I should be in much worse shape than I am—broken bones, torn muscles, or even internal injuries. Instead, I feel pretty much normal. Maybe even better than normal—more energetic than I've felt for a few years."

Kalrind smiled at him again.

"It isn't strange at all, Jim. It's a by-product of the Great Peace. Ever since then, you see, our researchers and yours have exchanged scientific data freely. The way I understand it, comparative biology has benefited especially. So our joint medical technology has advanced, accelerated enormously during the last century. That's why our doctors were able to heal you so quickly and so thoroughly."

Kalrind leaned forward and grasped Kirk's hand and spoke with great earnestness. "Do you understand, Jim? That's just one aspect of what's so wonderful about the Great Peace. It changed my whole civilization completely. It was the most important single event in Klingon history. It must be safeguarded."

Kirk was uncomfortably aware of her strong hand gripping his. "Are you saying it's in danger?"

Kalrind released his hand and leaned back in her seat again. "Later. We'll get to all of that later." She seemed suddenly subdued, even a bit sad. "That's for Morith to explain." Then her mood changed again. She sprang to her feet. "We'll worry about that later. Right now, I'm going to show you your new world. Come on!" She leaned forward, grasped his hand again, and pulled him from his chair.

"You're as impetuous as your ancestors."

She grinned. "The Universe destroys the sluggard. Old Klingon proverb. They weren't entirely worthless, those people."

"We say, 'Time and tide wait for no man,' but the Old Klingons said 'destroy,' instead."

Kalrind nodded. "An unforgiving race, and so they saw the universe as unforgiving, too. Now, let's get moving! Kalrind doesn't wait for sluggards, either."

The base was big, and the two of them found much to see and explore. Kirk found two differences between this Klingon base and a Starbase of his day; the second of these was pleasing, but the first was depressing.

That was the strangeness he encountered in certain areas—a technical unfamiliarity. As Kalrind showed him places where technical work was being done, he was bewildered by what he saw—and depressed by his bewilderment.

After he and Kalrind had watched a group of Klingon technicians performing an unidentifiable task, he said to her, "You know, I expected everything to be advanced—a century ahead of what I know. So I can accept being puzzled. But I'm having trouble accepting just *how* advanced everything must be. I have no idea what those people were doing. It makes me wonder if I ever *will* be able to learn what people know now, ever be able to catch up. When I get back to my own people, I won't be qualified to captain a starship, or any kind of vehicle. I'll be a historical curiosity, a resource for historians, and that's all."

"Some things don't change, Jim," Kalrind said. "Administration, running things—that's still the same. People don't change, after all." She laughed. "Well, your people don't. Mine have, as you know. I'll bet you could still be useful to Starfleet that way."

Kirk grimaced. "Desk work. It took a hundred years, but it finally caught up with me again."

The difference that pleased him was the freedom they were being allowed: except for the hospital area and parts of the base where an ignorant and careless tourist could cause major damage, such as the power station, they roamed at will.

"It wasn't like this in my day," he marveled. "I don't just mean that a Klingon wouldn't have given freedom to wander on a Starbase. I mean that even I wouldn't have been: various places would still have been off limits."

"Well, you can thank the Great Peace, you're seeing all these 'wonders of the future,' " Kalrind said. "And don't forget this is just an outpost! We're roughing it, by the standards of Klinzhai. Why, back home, you'd see much more expensive equipment. But out here . . . well, the fact is, out here we get the leftovers. We're still not as rich as the Federation, so outposts like this just have to make do with what they can get. The best still has to be restricted to Klinzhai and the other central worlds. Someday I'll show you the heart of the Empire, and then you'll really be amazed."

"Klinzhai," Kirk muttered. Center of the enemy nation, wellspring of evil, a word with which to frighten children. How difficult it was, at times, to abandon those old attitudes. "You still call it an empire?" he asked, changing the subject.

"In name only. The old authoritarianism is long gone, but the legal forms haven't changed. We're really a parliamentary democracy now, a constitutional monarchy. That's a respectable enough tradition in human history, isn't it?" she asked with a trace of anxiety.

Kirk smiled at her, thoroughly disarmed. "Oh, yes. Very respectable. Some of my own ancestors, on one side—well, never mind about all of that."

"But I want to know about it, Jim! I want to know all about your family and your ancestors. It's all so fascinating! Tell me about your family, Jim."

Kirk's smile faded slowly. "My family . . . I used to have a brother. I was very close to him." He winced in remembered pain.

Kalrind put her hand gently on his shoulder. "Something has happened to him?"

Kirk stared off into space silently for a moment. At last he said, "Years ago, yes." He looked off to the side, avoiding Kalrind's gaze, but she moved her hand to his cheek and pressed until he looked at her.

"My brother's name was Sam. Actually, George Samuel, but we always called him Sam. A good man, a very good man, and a fine scientist. He was married to a wonderful woman named Aurelan. They were both killed on one of our colony planets."

"How terrible! I'm sorry I forced you to talk about it, Jim."

Kirk drew in and released a deep breath. "*Thank* you for getting me to talk about it." He laughed.

"You're damned good at human psychology, for a Klingon!"

"Did Sam and Aurelan have any children?" Kalrind asked.

Kirk nodded. "Their son, Peter." He smiled fondly at the thought of his nephew. "Pete's a good kid. He's a research biologist now, just like his father. From what I hear, he'll be even better at it than Sam was." And then the depression returned. "What am I saying? That was all a hundred years ago! Pete's probably long dead, already. I've even lost him—my last surviving family." *And my ship and my crew, my substitute family, too.*

"I won't allow this," Kalrind said firmly. "You said something about your ancestors and parliamentary democracy. I want to know all about them, Captain Kirk, so start talking!"

Kirk forced a smile and began to tell her about Abernathy Kirk, who sat in the Long Parliament under John Pym and later fought for his faith and his republican beliefs under the great Cromwell, only to be forced to flee to the New World colonies when the Stuart monarchy was restored to England in 1660.

And as Kirk talked, his old fascination with the history of his family and his world took over, his depression lifted, and soon he was lecturing a smiling Kalrind with enthusiasm.

Chapter Five

"WELL, SPOCK, they all made it," McCoy said testily, reluctant to admit the truth to the Vulcan.

Spock nodded and turned to go.

"Wait a minute!" McCoy said. "Aren't you going to point out that you were right to do what you did? Crow a little?"

Spock raised an eyebrow. "I can see no point in doing so, Doctor. It would not give me the satisfaction it would give a human, and it would not prevent you from behaving in the future in the same dense and obstructionist fashion." He left the cramped office McCoy had been using since *Enterprise* had arrived at Starbase Seventeen.

McCoy watched him go and then muttered, "Well, it would give *me* satisfaction to crow over *your* mistakes, if I ever got the chance."

Spock had stopped at McCoy's office on his way to an appointment with Commodore Hellenhase, the commander of Starbase Seventeen. For many hours, he had been reevaluating his choice to continue to the Starbase at a low warp speed. His unemotional pose when explaining himself to McCoy aboard *Enterprise* had been only a pose; in fact, Spock had gone about his duties constantly aware that some among the injured might die, and it would be his fault. Wouldn't Jim Kirk, with his logic-defying intuitive leaps, have come up with some better course of action, some brilliant compromise, a middle path between excruciating alternatives?

Spock was relieved to hear that no one had died after all. Not only was a moral weight lifted from his shoulders, but also he could finally concentrate on regaining his normal Vulcan equilibrium, on becoming the controlled, logical being he pretended to be in front of McCoy.

Hellenhase was in his office waiting for Spock. The commodore was a man of medium height, slender, with hair so blond it was almost white. He was a serious, reserved man usually, but today even Spock could detect signs of distress.

He waved Spock into his office. "Come in, come in. Close the door. Now, listen, Spock, I've read the transcript of your message yesterday over and over again, and I just can't understand what happened. Oh, I understand what you described," he said, holding up his hand to prevent Spock from launching into a repetition of the report he had sent to Starfleet Command and Hellenhase after Kirk and *Mauler*'s disappearance, "but I don't see what it means. What's your opinion?"

"Insufficient data, Commodore. We know only that the Tholians disclaim all knowledge of the incident and that our sensor readings are quite different from those obtained when *Defiant* was destroyed in the same place. I would say this was not the same phenomenon as at that time, but rather something quite new."

"That means we're helpless to get Kirk back, then?"

Spock hesitated and then said, "At the moment, yes. However, it's our lack of data that cripples us, and therefore I feel it is imperative that we expend great efforts to gather more data in the area. I must once again urge—"

"Yes, yes, Spock," Hellenhase interrupted. "As you did yesterday. I won't say I disagree with you, even though Starfleet Command does. Send ships in to roam the area and uncover whatever they can. Except that we don't even know what to look for. We could just issue a warning to Federation ships to avoid that area from now on. Solve the problem that way."

"True, Commodore. But we have a Starfleet captain and a top-rated Security team missing, perhaps because of natural causes and perhaps not, and we would be shirking our duty to the Federation if we did less than we're able to."

Hellenhase stared at him penetratingly for a moment. "Hmph. I get your point, of course. The Tholians. Hmm. They'll be their usual touchy selves, of course. But we're making progress with them. Have to put all of that to the test, and a lot sooner than the Federation might have wished. And I suppose you want to be assigned to one of those ships so that you can be on the spot, eh?"

"I would, sir, but I would also like to stay with *Enterprise* while she undergoes repairs. And also with the crew while they are cared for here. Captain Kirk relinquished command to me, sir."

"The Vulcan sense of duty. Not always entirely logical, is it?" Spock chose not to answer.

Hellenhase waited a few seconds for a reply and

then gave up. "All right, all right, Spock. I'll get in touch with Starfleet Command right away and see what I can arrange." He waved a dismissal. As he watched Spock go, Hellenhase thought again of the Vulcan sense of duty. *And yet,* he told himself, *where would Starfleet be without it, eh?*

He said to his desk, "Get me Chung. In San Francisco."

A computer voice replied from his desk. "Power usage curve projections show that such a call would best be placed in five point two hours."

Hellenhase shook his head in exasperation. Vulcans and computers! One couldn't out-argue them, so one had to intimidate them. "Since I'm a commodore and you're a computer, I would say that the call would best be placed right now, when I asked for it!"

"Yes, Commodore," the computer replied meekly. "Although," the supposedly emotionless voice replied with unmistakable smugness, "it *is* just after two A.M. in San Francisco . . ."

Hellenhase grimaced. *The damned machine's right, of course.* He should have done the mental subtraction himself and figured that out. *Just shows how dealing with Vulcans fouls up my sense of time and everything else.* "All right, all right. Wait for nine hours and then place the call. And," he groaned, "when you get Chung, call my quarters and wake me up."

Officially, it was the Devonshire Excavation. Locals called it the Devon Ditch and the Devon Deeps, deliberately implying something dark and sinister down there, a gateway to demonic nether regions. Tourists from outside the area, even from off Earth, usually called it the Hole. That was all one needed to say: no one ever confused it with two other similarly named tourist attractions, the Great Hole of Kimberley or the site of the Black Hole of Calcutta, even though all three were man-made.

Unlike such natural excavations as the Grand Canyon or the Fish River Canyon or Mariner Valley, the sides of the Hole were not vertical. Even though there was a sturdy fence just past the observation platform to keep tourists from descending into the Hole, in fact the walls of it sloped down at a gentle angle and walking down into it would have been easy and without danger. But that would have robbed the place of its mystery and sinister air, and that would not have been good for tourism, and hence it was forbidden. Luisa Tindall longed to walk down into it.

"Nothing," she said. "It'd be nothing. We could get down there in a couple of hours or so and be back up before dark. We made much more strenuous hikes in the Rockies during our vacation, and that was at a much higher altitude."

"Aah, you passionate, impetuous Latins," Elliot said.

Luisa vindicated his use of the first adjective by stamping her foot angrily. "*Seriously,* Elliot! Why do you have to joke about everything? Is that because you're English?"

Elliot pondered the question. "I suppose the only thing we English are consistently serious about is the inferior races. Like Panamanians." He dodged the punch she aimed at his arm.

"I said I'm being serious!"

"I know you are, my little Spanish spitfire. Sorry: Panamanian *pimienta.*"

Luisa burst out laughing. "Damn you, Elliot. You always do that to me when I'm feeling serious."

"I don't like serious feelings," Elliot said—quite seriously. "They make me nervous."

"I've noticed that." Luisa was a short woman, and she had to crane her neck to look up at her husband. She wore her thick black hair in a single long braid down her back because Elliot loved it that way. She had never imagined that she could feel about anyone the way she felt about the enigmatic Englishman she had married two years earlier: so eager to know everything about him, to submerge herself in his life and interests and career.

But enigmas can lose their exotic charm as the years pass; they demand to be known, understood, explored. "But just look down there," Luisa said. "That's your past down there, your life. Don't you want to go down there and look for things, too?"

"No," Elliott said with unusual brusqueness. "There's nothing down there, Luisa. It was all vaporized when the *Golden Hind* hit. Oh, you're right, we could hike down there easily, if the authorities permitted it. But what do you think we'd find? Maybe you think we'd be able to stroll through the village I grew up in. Sorry." He shook his head. "That's all gone. There's *nothing* down there, Luisa, nothing. Not the school, or the church, or the manor house, or the cottages—nothing. Just a great big hole in the ground. The Devon Ditch: that's all there is."

Luisa grudgingly admitted the truth of that—at least, for the moment—and turned to look down into the Hole, huddling close against her husband, who held her tightly to him. Before her, the ground sloped downward into the deeps.

After eight years, the fertile soil and rainfall of England had already covered it with green. If you didn't know, she reflected, you would think it was natural. The walls of the famous Devon Hole looked gentle and grass-covered and inviting. Trees were growing on it—only saplings as yet, but in time they'd be enormous, masking from future eyes the disastrous origin of the Hole. Far below them was the bottom, devoid of grass or trees. Down there, she felt, as she had felt on every trip, down there was the truth, the essential nature of Elliot. Down there where the naked rock, the unvarnished foundation, of England was exposed—down there the soul of Elliot would be exposed. She wanted so desperately to find that soul. She looked away.

"Look over there," Luisa whispered delightedly to Elliot. He saw an elderly couple, both wearing brightly colored shorts, both aiming expensive cameras down into the Hole. Luisa said, "Aren't they the quintessential Americans? We're so different!"

Elliot smiled at her and said nothing.

"I thought you were Americans, too," a voice said.

Luisa turned and found herself face to face with a man of Elliot's age, dressed in a dull gray coverall, smiling in a friendly fashion. The man was obviously waiting for them to say something. "We're tourists," Elliot said.

"But not Americans?" He was a slender man, balding already, with light brown hair and a thin, open, friendly face.

"Yes, we are," Elliot said, obviously hoping the man would give up and go away.

"Ah, I see," the man said. "I'm a local. Used to be, I should say." He pointed down into the Hole. By now, the sun was setting, and the rocky bottom of the Hole, far below them, was in deep shadow. "I lived down there. There was a village, named Berton. I was away from home when it happened. Not quite twenty. My family was there when it happened, my whole family. And everyone I knew—all lost. Why, and the crew of the ship, too, of course. I rushed back when I heard the news, but . . ." He pointed again toward the Hole. "That's all I found. Still smoking, surrounded by ambulances which had nothing to do." He seemed to have forgotten them, to have become absorbed in the past hidden in the shadows filling the bottom of the Hole.

Luisa, her quick sympathy aroused, reached out toward the man's arm, but Elliot grabbed her hand and pulled it back. "We have to get back to San Francisco, dear. I'm past due." He began to walk swiftly away, pulling Luisa with him, leaving the oblivious survivor of the disaster still staring down into the Hole.

"I don't understand why you did that," Luisa said helplessly. "You always said Berton was such a small village. That man might have been someone you knew as a child. You should be delighted to meet him. You know we don't have to get back any time soon."

Elliot sighed and slowed his pace. "I *did* know him, and I hated his guts when we were both kids. Okay? He was pushy even then, and he seems to have grown worse. I thought all of them were dead. I hoped some of them were. Besides, we're strangers now. My friends aren't here anymore: they're in San Francisco."

They walked in silence for a while. Finally Luisa said, "Whatever you say, Elliot."

Elliot groaned. "Please, darling. I don't want to argue with you." His words were conciliatory, but

Luisa could sense his growing anger. "Let's get back to the boardinghouse," he said.

They spoke little to each other that evening.

Elliot went to bed early. When Luisa came into the bedroom later, she found the lights on. Elliot was sprawled on his back atop the covers, fully dressed and sleeping soundly. His mouth was open and he was snoring. The computer he had brought with him on the trip despite Luisa's objections lay on his chest, still turned on.

Luisa picked up the computer and glanced incuriously at the screen. Displayed on it was some sort of heavily technical article Elliot had been reading, something by a man named Spock. Luisa grimaced and turned the computer off. Then she began the job of getting Elliot undressed and under the covers. It pleased the maternal side of her whenever she had to do this—and it happened fairly often—but she was also aware of a small, nagging resentment because he was so heavy and difficult to maneuver.

She finished the task at last and sat down beside him on the bed. "Whew! Elliot," she muttered, "what would you do without me?" Gently, she brushed his hair back from his forehead, feeling under her fingertips the scars he still bore from a boyhood accident.

It had happened, she thought with a shiver at the eeriness of it all, a few miles away, down in what was now the Hole, where a whole village and its population had vanished in an instant. Years before that vast accident, her Elliot had smashed his forehead against a rock in a much smaller accident, a very individual and personal one. The great accident had scarred a nation; the minor one had left only scars hidden by a man's hair. But it was the smaller accident that touched her heart and made her feel fear in retrospect: how close her beloved husband had come to not living to adulthood, and therefore to not meeting and marrying her! How could his recent moodiness matter when set against that near-loss? She brushed her fingers across the scars again.

Chapter Six

THE KLINGON BASE was much like a starbase in function and form. Kirk was startled to find that it even had a recreation area designed to simulate an outdoor forest. Not that such an area was in itself a complete novelty to him. After all, *Enterprise* had the very same thing onboard. It was rather that, in spite of all he had seen and heard during the last few days of exploring, this was still not what he had expected on a Klingon base.

He and Kalrind were lying side by side on their backs on thick grass, staring up through tree branches at a blue sky across which small clouds moved slowly. Kirk pointed up. "That's really well done. All that's needed to complete the illusion is the drone of insects. I could just let myself go and drift off to sleep here. I wouldn't mind a nap."

Kalrind laughed. "From all I've read about your battles with my ancestors, I always pictured you as a much more energetic man." She sat up halfway, resting on one elbow, and looked down at him affectionately. "An unapproachable, mythological figure. A superhuman hero."

"I'm surprised your ancestors didn't leave you a

very different picture," Kirk said, smiling. "Someone very evil."

"They did, by their lights. Their records are as unflattering about you as they could be. They accused you of not possessing the martial virtues they admired. But that just makes you more appealing in New Klingon eyes. Also, we've learned to take their prejudices and distorted values into account when we read the old documents. We translate, in other words—not the language, but the attitudes."

"You seem to know your ancestors so well. Better than we humans know our own, I think."

"There are reasons for that. I'll explain them some time. For now, though, I'm more interested in you than in my ancestors." She leaned over him, staring down at him for a long moment.

At her closeness, that strong, dark, heavy-boned Klingon face, Kirk felt an instant of panic—a feeling of being a prey animal at a predator's mercy. Then that feeling faded, and Kalrind became Kalrind again, just herself and not a representative of anything or a type or a symbol.

She leaned down and kissed him softly.

"How gentle you are!" Kirk said. "Do all Klingons kiss that way?"

"You didn't like it?"

"Oh, yes, I did. Very much." He put his hand up and stroked her thick black hair. Klingon hairstyles hadn't changed much in the last one hundred years, he reflected.

"We're still stronger than human beings, you know. We just don't feel obligated to prove it all the time. Anyway, I'm not sure how recovered you are, Jim."

Kirk grinned. "I feel fine. Good as new."

Kalrind leaned down and kissed him again, harder

than before. This time her strength showed, and a hint of fierceness. He wasn't fully recovered, Kirk realized; at the moment she *was* stronger than he. Again, for an instant, Kirk felt afraid.

Later, as they lay sleepily in the warm air, Kirk realized that Kalrind's strength no longer frightened him, but the strength and depth of his own feelings did. He stroked her head, resting on his shoulder; it was a comforting weight. Kalrind stretched and sighed.

"I suppose," Kirk said, "New Klingons don't worry about being interrupted when they're doing something important."

Kalrind chuckled. "I gave orders. This place is ours all day."

Suddenly she stood and began pacing. Her expression was serious and thoughtful. "I read about you in history class when I was a girl. I used to daydream about the brave and gallant and handsome James T. Kirk . . . but I never daydreamed . . . anything like this." She glanced down at Kirk and then looked away again. "This all takes me by surprise."

"Me, too," Kirk said quietly, rising to his feet. He stood beside her and lowered his head to rest on her shoulder. How much of this powerful emotion he felt for Kalrind, he wondered, was actually a seeking after consolation and warmth, comfort for the loss of his universe? *Or am I asking myself this just because I feel guilty for loving a Klingon woman*? His grasp on reality was diminishing with the passing days, instead of growing as he grew to know his new world. He was disoriented, floating in a haze, a mist.

He had sagged against Kalrind until she was supporting his weight almost entirely. His legs felt unable to hold him.

"Jim! Jim!"

"What? Oh . . ." Shakily, he pushed himself away from her and leaned against a wall.

"You collapsed against me! You just went all limp."

He shook his head. "Sorry. You all right?"

"Of *course* I'm all right!" Kalrind snapped. "Are *you* all right?"

Nothing that a trip back in time wouldn't cure. "I'm feeling better now. Just a passing something-or-other."

Kalrind looked annoyed. "I want you examined."

"Really, Kalrind, I'm all right now."

"Nonsense! I'll talk to Morith about it."

"Your tone of command is very good."

"You won't joke me out of it, Jim. For now, though, I'm taking you back to our room so you can take a nap."

For a momnent, Kirk was inclined to argue. He had felt briefly that he was on the track of something important, some crucial, pivotal idea or self-perception. But then he decided that Kalrind was right and he needed a nap far more than introspection.

Kirk awoke enormously refreshed. He practically jumped from the wide bed, throwing the covers back so vigorously that they slid onto the floor. He showered and dressed in the simple blue tunic that he found draped over a chair in the room, and then, feeling suddenly tremendously hungry, he left the room and walked rapidly in the direction of the dining hall.

Kalrind was there, seated at a small table with Morith, deep in some serious discussion. Kirk approached their table from Kalrind's rear, intending to surprise her. But Morith saw him coming and said something to her, and she stopped talking and turned around. "Jim! You look recovered."

"Yep. I feel great. And starving." He went to a dispensing machine against one wall and returned with a loaded tray.

Morith smiled. "Don't overdo it, Jim. I doubt if we have any spare human stomachs in stock on the base."

Kirk shook his head. "Plenty of room for this. And then I want to do some more exploring. Or maybe go to the gym for a workout. I have so much energy all of a sudden, I don't know how to get rid of it all."

"I have a minor crisis to put down," Morith said, rising. "I suspect a doctor would recommend exploring over working out for you at this stage, Jim."

Remembering his episode of weakness earlier in the day, Kirk nodded. "You're probably right, Morith. Exploration it will be. You'll come with me, won't you, Kalrind?"

"Sorry." She stood up. "Morith's crisis is my problem, too. Besides, I'm feeling tired. I think I'll go to bed early. You'll have to wander around on your own."

Kirk waved goodbye as she left; his mouth was too full to talk. His hunger was overwhelming. He kept swallowing and then stuffing his mouth again, and even so it took some time before he began to feel satisfied. *Strange thing, this hunger*, he thought. *It's almost as if my collapse earlier today and then the nap constituted some sort of adjustment crisis, and now my body is ready to go in this new time, to rebuild and press forward. That's why it needs so much energy. I wonder if that makes any sense? I ought to ask Bones . . .*

He caught himself in time and sternly shook off the wave of sadness and loss. McCoy and Spock and the others, and *Enterprise* itself: it was done, it was finished, it was a fact of life, a new fact of life, and he would have to live with it, would have to adjust. *And I* will, he promised himself. He had always prided himself on his ability to adjust, and there had even been times when he had saved his own life and the lives of others through that ability. Now that not only his life but his sanity was at stake, how could he let himself fail?

His age, his century, his civilization—they were all gone. *This* was now his universe. The fact was irreversible. So be it. *I will adjust*.

And right now, he would explore.

He finished his last plateful of food, returned dishes, glass, and utensils to the recycler, and left the dining hall.

About an hour later, Kirk's urge to explore was rewarded.

He was in a long, featureless hallway with few doors. As he strode along impatiently, eager to find something more interesting, a door ahead of him opened and a brilliant light flooded out of it. *Well*, Kirk thought, *this might be something different*. Shielding his eyes from the glare, he headed for the open door—but slowly and cautiously.

A glowing sphere drifted through the doorway and into the corridor. A great echoing voice filled the corridor. "Greetings, James Kirk, and welcome to the future."

"An Organian!" Kirk exclaimed.

"Correct, Captain Kirk, an Organian." The light shimmered and moved closer to him. "We have met before, Kirk."

"I've only met Organians once before, on Organia itself."

"Indeed. You knew me there as Ayleborne, chairman of the Council of Elders. I spoke to you and Kor, the Old Klingon. Kor considered himself governor of my world, which he termed a newly acquired outpost of the Klingon Empire, and you and Mr. Spock considered yourselves freedom fighters, obligated to liberate us from Klingon domination." The Organian's voice had assumed an amused tone.

Kirk smiled. "I've always thought of Organians as humorless beings, not given to sarcasm."

"We have had to change ourselves over the last century, in order to deal more effectively with your people and the Klingons. I'm here on a brief visit—then I will travel to Earth to meet the leaders of your Federation. Fortunately, because of the Great Peace, we have served in a liaison capacity, rather than as policemen. Do you remember, Kirk, how you reacted when I predicted the Great Peace?"

"Yes. I remember that I didn't believe you."

"Indeed you didn't. I'm not sure who was more skeptical, you or Kor. The two of you were quite sure that violence and hatred between your two races must continue forever."

"Perhaps not forever," Kirk said. "I always thought peace was possible. I just didn't see any likelihood of it anytime soon."

"And now?"

"Apparently I was wrong. What you predicted has happened."

"I'm gratified to hear you admit that, Kirk. Now I must leave you. But I will be returning to this base. Perhaps we will find time to speak again." The brilliant sphere floated back through the doorway, and the door began to close.

"Wait!" Kirk called out, as he ran to the door, which slid shut just as he got there. He knocked and called out repeatedly, but the door remained closed.

There were so many questions he had been saving for years in case he met an Organian again! Now he wondered how much longer they would remain unanswered. He had once said sarcastically, "There's never an Organian around when you need one." This new situation was even more frustrating. Dissatisfied, he turned and began to make his way back toward his room.

That night, Kirk was possessed by dreams of pursuit and capture, imprisonment and torture. He was surrounded by Old Klingon faces, some of which he knew, malevolent faces leering down at him as he lay strapped to an operating table and Klingon knives dug into him.

He awoke sweating and shaking. Kalrind was holding him tightly. "Jim! You were calling your ship for help. What was it?"

"Nothing," he muttered, "Just an old nightmare." Comforted by her presence, he sank back into an uneasy sleep.

In the morning Kirk awoke, feeling drained. He soon realized that his weakness was more than inadequate rest. It was something more fundamental than that. He could barely drag himself about the base, just as he had felt on first emerging from unconsciousness among the new Klingons.

Though he tried to avoid Kalrind and pretended to be as energetic as the day before, she was not that easily fooled. That evening in the dining hall, Morith joined them. "So, Jim," he said, "Kalrind tells me that you're having some physical problems."

"Me? Why, no, how did she get that impression?"

"For one thing," Kalrind said, "right now you're

finding it a real effort to raise your fork to your mouth and to keep your eyes open."

"I didn't sleep too well last night," Kirk admitted.

"Those nightmares of yours worry me. And your weakness," Morith said.

Kirk turned to Kalrind. "Do you tell Morith everything?"

"Not quite everyting."

"Well, that's something to be thankful for."

"I want you to check back into the hospital," Morith persisted. "Our doctors should check into this."

Kirk lacked the energy to object.

That night, instead of returning to the room he shared with Kalrind, he went to the hospital with Morith. There he was shown into the same room in which he had found himself days before and ordered to undress and get into the bed. A Klingon he thought he recognized from his first, brief awakening appeared, nodded at him, and applied an instrument to his arm. *Hypospray,* Kirk thought. *Guess some things haven't been improved in a hundred years. Bones would have been amused. . . .* The drug took effect and Kirk entered a dreamless sleep.

"The doctors can't find anything wrong," Morith assured him the next day. "Your body's healed. It must be some sort of psychological phenomenon resulting from your injuries. Unfortunately, human psychology is not a field we have much expertise in, so there's not much more we can say. You seem fine now, though."

"Brimming with energy again," Kirk assured him. "I'd prefer to forget about it until and unless it happens again."

Morith grinned. "That's the sort of optimistic attitude doctors like."

Kalrind was more upset than Kirk, even though she tried to hide her feelings from him. Kirk was touched by her concern, but he had other and more immediate worries, one of which was the chance that his latest burst of energy might be short-lived and that he must use it while it lasted. The other appeared while he was capitalizing upon his renewed energy and trying to see and learn everything he could about this future time.

On the afternoon of his new recovery, Kirk and Kalrind were at a window overlooking a gymnasium, watching off-duty Klingons engaging in strenuous recreation. Kalrind tried to pull him away, to get him to look at some other part of the base with her, but Kirk had stopped in fascination to watch the scene below.

The floor of the gymnasium was covered with three sets of parallel lines, so that the surface was tiled with variously colored triangles. The Klingons, all stripped to the waist and sweating heavily, seemed to be following complicated rules governing which triangle each could be in and how they were allowed to move between them. There was much wrestling and shoving and even rather vicious-looking kicks and punches.

"Hard-hitting game," Kirk remarked, pointing to a group in one corner, who were either resting or disqualified, he wasn't sure which. Bruises and red streaks showed on their skins. "Looks a bit like *klin zha*."

Kalrind looked distressed at the reference. "You know about *klin zha*? I thought humans of your time knew nothing of that."

"Most of us didn't," Kirk agreed. "I read a book about Klingons that described the game, though. I'm surprised to see New Klingons still doing it."

"Yes." Kalrind nodded. "Yes, you're right. Anyone else on this base would drop the subject immediately if you raised it, and I have to confess that it makes me uneasy, too. You see, there are some things from our past that we seem unable to drop. It's as if that part of us still survives, on some level. Oh, we try to pretend that we've purged ourselves of it, the way Vulcans have purged themselves of their violent past, but I think we're lying about it a little bit."

Kirk laughed. "Just like Vulcans, although even my friend Mr. Spock would have come close to a fit if he had heard me say that." He returned his attention to the gym floor. "Seems to work, though. They're all in good shape, and it's hard to keep your people that way on space duty without some sort of motivation, something that'll make them get into the gym regularly and work hard. If your version of *klin zha* does that trick, then there's no reason to complain."

From behind him, a harsh voice said, "Of course there's reason to complain!"

Kirk turned around to face the dark, angry face of Klanth. Instead of the Klingon officer's uniform of a hundred years earlier, he wore a tunic, identical to those worn by Kalrind and Morith and the other New Klingons. And yet on Klanth, the tunic seemed out of place, foreign. He radiated the hostility and barely contained anger Kirk knew so well. He was unchanged; he was the Klanth of old. Kalrind pressed against Kirk—whether to seek protection or offer it, Kirk couldn't tell.

"You're not happy in this century, Klanth?" Kirk said mildly, tensing himself for an attack.

Klanth moved forward, but his object was not Kirk or Kalrind. Instead he stepped up to the window. When he spoke, his voice was calmer and thoughtful. "How could a true Klingon be happy here? Look at them." He pointed through the window. "How can you dignify that with the name *klin zha*? A Klingon child of my day could defeat any of them in hand-to-hand combat. Even you could, Kirk. Are these the heirs of the Klingon Empire? Is this what I and my fellow Klingons fought and sacrificed so much for—so that these weaklings and cowards could inherit our power?'' He shook his head. ''I have more in common with you than I do with them.''

''Is that past something to mourn for?'' Kirk asked. ''We were warriors, Captain, and our day is over. They don't need us any more. The Galaxy is a peaceful place, now. Our kind of man—''

''Rubbish!'' Klanth shouted, his face darkening still further. His moment of thoughtfulness had passed, and he was once again the fierce Old Klingon warrior. ''Do you think I'm going to let this continue? They killed my crew, Kirk!''

Kalrind stepped in front of Kirk. ''Your crew were killed by the storm and the stress of the time jump. The same thing happened to Captain Kirk's men. At least some of *yours* survived, Captain Klanth. You should strive to be happy at their survival, and not give way to anger. We can help you—''

Klanth bellowed and lunged at her. Kirk grabbed her tunic and pushed her aside. She stumbled out of Klanth's way, and the Klingon collided with Kirk. Both men fell heavily to the floor, Klanth on top.

The Klingon reached for Kirk's throat. Kirk tried to bring his arms up, to sweep Klanth's hands out of the way, but his strength suddenly drained away and he could not move because of Klanth's weight.

Suddenly Klanth went limp.

The Klingon captain was dragged off Kirk and thrown to the floor. ''Jim!'' It was Kalrind, fear in her eyes as she bent over Kirk's unmoving body.

"I'm all right," he muttered. "Help me . . ."

She helped him sit up and then supported him as he climbed to his feet. "Knocked the breath out of me, that's all," he said, smiling to reassure her. It was a lie, but it was true that his strength was returning slowly.

Kirk became aware that the corridor was crowded with Klingons, Morith among them, and that some of the Klingons were holding weapons trained on Klanth and three others. Looking at them more closely, Kirk realized that the three men under guard bore the marks of the Old Klingon that he had noticed in Klanth—the glaring eyes, the rage-darkened face. Those signs were much clearer to him, now that he could see Old and New Klingons together.

Morith said to the Klingons with him, "Keep careful watch over these—animals." Then he stepped over to Kirk and said, "Jim, you don't look too good. Perhaps we ought to have you checked again."

Kirk waved his hand and repeated his earlier lie. "Klanth knocked the wind out of me. I'll be all right in a few minutes. What's the story with those men?"

Morith grimaced. "Klanth's surviving crewmembers. They're just like him. They saw a fight getting started, and they rushed to join in. Animals." He looked as if he had swallowed something foul. "We thought we could bring them up to our standard, and we've been trying, but . . ." He gestured helplessly.

"They're a danger to you, aren't they?"

Morith nodded soberly. "They'll never fit in. Not in our part of the Empire, anyway. We don't know how to deal with these people; we never have. Our history hasn't prepared us for this." He smiled crookedly. "You know, Jim, the irony is that my ancestors would have had no problem dealing with these people. Well, not these people, of course, but people whom they considered a danger. For them, the solution would have been simple and obvious. Our higher morality condemns us to a more complicated solution."

Kirk was feeling far stronger by now. He was able to stand without any help from Kalrind. "So what solution have you chosen?"

"When the next transport passes by, we're going to load Klanth and his men onto it and send them back to Klinzhai. Possibly the medical experts there can do something with them. We've been making great strides in drug therapy lately. We can now help the sick, the brain-damaged—and that's what I consider Klanth and his men to be. If they can't be helped in that way . . ." his voice trailed off.

"Come on, Jim," Kalrind said, taking his hand. "Let's go back to your quarters."

After that incident, Kirk saw no more of Klanth or any of his men. He was relieved, yet a part of him brooded: Klanth had been right to say that he and Kirk were of a kind, and that as warriors, they were unique in this age.

Years earlier, Kirk had read one of the personal testaments remaining from one of Earth's great wars of the age before spaceflight. The writer had said that he and his fellow soldiers had more in common with the enemy soldiers than with his own country's civilians. The only men who could really understand him, he had written, were those who marched with him and those they fought against. Only they had shared the grim life he had been living throughout the years of combat, and no civilian on either side could ever understand what those men had been through.

Struck by that, Kirk had sought out other such

books to learn if soldiers from many countries and many times had felt the same. Kirk had realized, reading those old books, that he felt that way as well. And now Klanth had said it aloud.

The brotherhood of warriors, Kirk thought. *Only warriors understand it—are even aware of it.* Perhaps Klanth and his kind were indeed the beasts Kalrind and Morith said they were. Perhaps they were unpredictable and dangerous, but Kirk would have given anything to talk of these matters with the Old Klingon, a product of his own century, that proud and solitary warrior from his own time.

Chapter Seven

SPOCK HAD CERTAINLY NOT LIED to Commodore Hellenhase about his desire to stay at Starbase Seventeen with *Enterprise* while she underwent repairs. Indeed, Kirk had relinquished the con to him, and Spock therefore felt that his place was with Kirk's ship until all was well with it again. As the ranking officer he also felt it was his duty to stay with the crew while they recovered from the psychological wounds resulting from the loss of their captain. In cases such as that of Uhura, there were physical wounds as well.

But while Spock had not lied about his motivations, his subsequent actions converted his words to Hellenhase into a lie. The few times he had tried to associate with the crew, he had found it no easier than it had ever been—worse, in fact. Their general hostility to him resulted from his decision to leave the area of Kirk's disappearance and continue to Starbase Seventeen.

Spock, unable to ignore their feelings, had realized that, under those conditions, his presence was of no benefit to them. Combined with the lure of investigation, the intellectual zeal that was one of the few emotions Vulcans admired, this was enough to make him surrender, to give up the unrewarded effort to socialize with the crew, and retire to the nearest available computer workstation.

And it was here that Mr. Scott found him.

"Good afternoon, Mr. Spock," *Enterprise*'s chief engineer said happily. "I've been searching for you high and low. There's major work to be done on my engines, and I'd very much like your input."

"*Your* engines, Mr. Scott?" the Vulcan said, not taking his eyes from his monitor screen.

"Call 'em what you will, Mr. Spock," the engineer said in annoyance, "but to my mind they're my own personal possessions."

Spock sighed in resignation and turned away from a graph displayed in front of him. "Indeed. I am at your disposal, Mr. Scott. What did you wish to ask me?"

The engineer's annoyance vanished, and eagerness took its place. "Well, you see, Mr. Spock, it's like this. We have to do a major rebuilding of the matter-antimatter containment vessel. Now, while we were away, some important new developments have taken place. We could reconstruct the vessel just as it was before, or we could modify it to deliver much more power in short bursts. During warp acceleration, for example. I think that would be a real benefit."

"I assume there's a drawback. Otherwise you would not have needed my advice or concurrence."

"Aye," Scott said unhappily. "You see, the new design draws greater power at all other times and would therefore decrease shield power and normal life-support reserves. Apparently, some ships have even reported lower impulse power; there shouldn't be any relationship, but apparently there is."

"Then the decision seems clearcut to me. Obviously we cannot afford such an improvement."

"Ah, but it's a marvelous improvement, Mr. Spock! I could even call it a breakthrough. I'd be delighted to put it in place."

"Nevertheless, Mr. Scott, it is clearly impractical. In my experience, *Enterprise* needs shield power, life-support reserves, and impulse power far more often than she needs greater warp acceleration."

"Aye," Scott said sadly. "I thought the same, but I was hoping that you'd be able to see a reason to put the new system in place."

One Vulcan eyebrow rose. "I have never understood why humans so often wish to be argued out of a course of action that their own judgment reveals to be the best one."

"No," the engineer said, "I don't suppose you would understand that, Mr. Spock. However, there's another reason I came looking for you. Access codes and passwords, damn them."

"You are far too cryptic, Mr. Scott."

"I'm talking about the computers on our ship, Mr. Spock."

"I understood that," the Vulcan said patiently. "What I cannot understand is you need to damn computer codes and passwords." He might have asked in what sense such immaterial objects *could* be damned, but over the years, he had learned about humans' and use of idioms and their annoyance when questioned too closely about them.

"I have to change them all!" Scott exploded. "Hour upon hour of work. It's taking me forever, and it's time I need to be spending on the engines and the structure of the ship instead. Since you're such a computer expert, Mr. Spock, I hoped you might show me how to speed the process up."

"Mr. Scott, the process you are now using was designed by Starfleet for optimal speed. Aren't you really asking me for permission to bypass the process and leave some access codes and passwords unchanged?" He stared coolly at the engineer.

Scott shamefaced, refused to meet the First Officer's eye. "A stupid waste of time," he muttered. "A stupid rule."

"You know better than than, Mr. Scott," the Vulcan said. A hint of sternness had crept into Spock's normally unemotional voice. "Starfleet regulations specify that access codes and passwords and ship dispositions are to be changed throughout the fleet following the disappearance of an officer of the rank and position of Captain Kirk."

Scott sighed. "Aye, Mr. Spock, I know of that rule. And I haven't argued with it when we knew that the lost man was in the hands of the enemy. But that's simply not the case here! We know what happened to the captain: he was caught in a space storm of some kind and thrown into another space, and that's where he still is."

"I tend to agree with you," Spock admitted, "but we cannot prove that; we cannot be sure. Until we are, we must assume the worst. We must operate under the assumption that Captain Kirk is in the hands of an enemy, either one we know or one we don't, and that he has been drugged or tortured until he has told his captors everything he knows about Starfleet."

Scott shook his head. "I'd never believe that about the captain."

Spock resolutely changed the subject. "How are the repairs progressing, Mr. Scott?"

"Oh, on schedule in spite of this computer nonsense. She'll be as good as new in a couple of weeks. Even better, in some respects."

"Excellent. What about Commander Uhura's console?"

Scott threw up his hands in an expression of frustration and paced energetically about the small space near Spock's chair. The Vulcan watched him with a detached, analytical air. "I can't figure that one out at all, Mr. Spock. Those consoles are very heavily insulated! No one gets shocked by them—not unless there's been major physical damage, and in this case there wasn't."

"Dr. McCoy insists that Commander Uhura did indeed suffer a severe electrical shock, however. She was rendered unconscious by that and not by being thrown around subsequently, as we all were."

Scott winced at the memory and touched his head gingerly. "Och, aye. Some of us will bear the marks of that shaking for months. It's so much easier to repair a ship than a human being. But then, ships are more logically designed."

"I'm surprised to hear a human admit that," Spock said approvingly. "Commander Uhura was lucky to survive the shock, even luckier that she has recovered fully, with no aftereffects. The next crewman exposed to such a shock might not be so fortunate."

"I *know* that, Mr. Spock! I canna perform miracles! I dinna ken the reason!" The engineer breathed deeply and calmed himself down. "All my tests and simulations reveal nothing, no cause for what happened. Same applies to the data recordings from the internal console sensors."

"I have examined the same recordings, Mr. Scott, and I concur. However, I have also examined the recordings of the incoming subspace signals Commander Uhura was monitoring during that time." He gestured at the monitor in front of him.

Scott leaned over to look at the display. He noticed the plain, white cover of a Starfleet technical report next to the keyboard and picked it up. "Elliot Tindall," he muttered. "I've heard good things about the man, but I've never been able to understand his stuff."

"Fortunately, however, I do," Spock said smoothly, taking the thick report from the engineer's hand and putting it down again, outside the human's reach. "The monitor, Mr. Scott."

Scott returned his attention to the display. "I can't see what good that will do, Mr. Spock. There's no information contained in those signals that'll tell us anything about malfunctions in the equipment."

"Quite true, Mr. Scott. I'm searching these recordings for something outside the equipment. And I believe I have found it."

There was a pause, which Scott was convinced was calculated for dramatic effect. He quickly lost his temper. "Well, spit it oot, mon!"

"I have found evidence," Spock continued calmly, "that the electric shock was caused by a very short but very powerful signal which overloaded the console's damping circuits and its monitoring subsystems. That signal was carried on the frequency which Commander Uhura was using to monitor the transponder Captain Kirk took with him when he transported to *Mauler*."

The engineer stopped pacing and stared at the Vulcan. "Aye," he said thoughtfully, "that's possible. But what could have caused such a signal, Mr. Spock? It would have to be tremendously powerful."

"Indeed it would," Spock said thoughtfully. "But I

need more data about it before I can draw any conclusions. I will require some highly classified Starfleet equipment, to which I do not normally have access."

"Ah! So that's why you've been down here on the base instead of up on the ship during its repairs."

"Exactly," Spock said. "I needed the computer power available on the Starbase. I filed my reports to Starfleet Command by means of subspace radio."

"That must have made them happy." Scott added a chuckle.

"Not at all, Mr. Scott. They were most unhappy. However, they bowed to my logic when I pointed out that here I could both have access to sufficient computer power and be close to the ship in case I was needed."

"And you were!" Scott said eagerly. "You've helped me greatly, and you just did it again today."

"Quite true. I have reached the point, however, where I must have access to the classified equipment I mentioned, and I have been informed that it is currently under guard at Starfleet Headquarters."

"Earth!" Scott said. "Well, I wouldn't mind a vacation in the old country myself, Mr. Spock, but I don't like going to that world on business."

"I share your distaste," Spock said gravely. "However, I can see no choice. I will be leaving Starbase Seventeen for Earth late this evening. I expect to return well before *Enterprise* is once again spaceworthy."

"She's always spaceworthy, Mr. Spock," the engineer said reprovingly. "Just more so sometimes than others."

"Let us say, then, that I should be back before *Enterprise* once again meets your exacting engineering standards, Mr. Scott."

The engineer beamed at him. "Aye, now *that* I can accept!" He left the room whistling.

Spock watched him go with an impassive face. A curious species, the human one. He suspected he would study it for years without understanding it. He turned his attention back to his computer terminal.

Chapter Eight

"THINK YOU'RE WELL ENOUGH for classes, Jim?"
Kirk looked at her questioningly. They were back in the base's park; it had become their favorite place to relax and talk. And relaxing was what Kirk was doing. Kalrind was sitting crosslegged next to him, and he was lying on his back, stretched out, chewing lazily on a blade of grass.

"Haven't you ever wondered what I do, what my career is?" Kalrind asked him.

"I suppose I just assumed your whole duty in life was to keep me happy."

Kalrind grinned. "Am I succeeding?"

"Admirably. I'm going to recommend you for a medal."

"Actually, I'm here for a serious purpose."

"You know," Kirk told her, "I've noticed one way in which you New Klingons are very much like your ancestors."

Kalrind drew away from him. She frowned, her heavy brows forming a V, her dark forehead wrinkling. Suddenly, she looked dangerous, an unsettling echo of her racial past. "Oh?"

Kirk forced a laugh. "Yes. Like them, you don't have much of a sense of humor."

Kalrind relaxed again. "I think you're right," she said very seriously, and went on to prove Kirk's point. "It's a failing on our part. We should strive to develop a sense of humor. I think it has value."

Kirk shook his head but decided to change the subject. "So. You were about to tell me about the serious reason you have for being here."

"Yes. Of course. My training is in the study of history. As soon as we realized who you were, I was brought to the base. You were still unconscious at the time."

"I can understand your coming here," Kirk said. "Klanth and his surviving crewmen are a boon. You must have been eager to question them."

"Klanth!" Kalrind said scornfully. "Might as well try to interrogate a *Qatlh pub,* or some other wild animal. No, Jim, these Old Klingons are worthless creatures. I'm not sure they even think the way I do. What I meant was that *you personally* brought me here. You are our historical resource."

"You mean the Federation hasn't given you complete records from my era, so that you can learn about it?"

Kalrind smiled at him fondly. "You're being obtuse, Jim. It's not your era that we want to know about: it's you."

"Aah, of course. The gallant, legendary hero."

But Kalrind didn't respond with a smile or a laugh, as Kirk had expected. "That's right, Jim."

Now Kirk sat up. "I'm ready," he said quietly. "Tell me everything you know."

"Let's walk," Kalrind said. "Sitting still for so long makes me edgy."

As they strolled between the thick-boled trees, Kalrind continued, "A few days ago, you said that you kept hearing about the Tholian Incident, but you didn't know what it was. Now I will tell you.

"One hundred years ago, there was a confrontation between two great fleets, one Klingon, one Starfleet. They were facing each other across the frontier between their two spheres of influence. It was very near where you and *Mauler* were caught by the storm and thrown forward to our own time, and only four weeks after that happened."

"Near Tholia," Kirk said.

"Exactly. Hence the name, the Tholian Incident."

"And the Tholians didn't interfere?" Kirk asked. "We found them to be rather touchy about their territory."

"Considering the combined size of the two fleets, I suppose the Tholians decided they'd be better off not getting involved."

"They had that strange technology, though," Kirk recalled. "That web of theirs . . ."

"Yes," Kalrind said. "But consider the energies if the two fleets had had a battle. I doubt if even the Tholian web could have stood up to it. And it certainly looked like a battle was about to break out."

"Then the Organians should have done something. Lord knows, they were certainly busybodies back then."

Kalrind stepped off the pathway and sat down in the grass, leaning against a tree. She patted the ground beside her. Kirk joined her. "Since the Organians seemed to know what everyone was up to, they must have known that the Klingons were on a diplomatic mission and not an attack. They were New Klingons."

"But we never heard anything about New Klingons,

in my time," Kirk protested. "If they already existed back then, we would have wanted to get in contact with them."

"Imperial politics, Jim. The Old Klingons were still firmly in control of the Empire, and whenever they found any of my ancestors, they either imprisoned or killed them. The first New Klingons had to operate underground. Even so, there were apparently enough of them hidden in command positions to scrape together that fleet and head for the Federation frontier to make peace with your people. The records are incomplete."

"And so that's how the Great Peace came about?" Kirk said.

"That *should* have been how it came about, but your people didn't trust the New Klingons. They refused to believe that there *was* such a thing as a New Klingon, and they were sure the whole thing was just a Klingon trick."

"A reasonable assumption."

Kalrind nodded. "Given what they knew about Klingons, yes. So the confrontation continued while the New Klingons tried to convince the Federation fleet commanders about who and what they were, and the Federation people's trigger fingers got itchier and itchier." She gripped his arm fiercely. "The Klingons had come to initiate peace, and instead they were on the verge of starting interstellar war!

"Even the New Klingons would defend themselves if the Federation ships attacked them. Once the shooting started, you can imagine how impossible diplomacy would have been. It would have meant war. And not only would that lead to death and destruction on both sides, it would also have destroyed the New Klingon position within the Empire."

"Doesn't sound like they had much of a position."

"I suppose not. Let's say that with peace, they would have been strengthened and gained a position. In fact, that's exactly what happened: the New Klingons used the peace treaty as a wedge to get into positions of power and start taking over the Empire. But a war might have led to their total elimination. The Organians might have intervened, but they didn't show any signs of doing so."

"So there was a stalemate between the two fleets. What broke it?"

"You did!" she said. "The records from both sides show that Captain James Kirk, *aboard a Klingon ship,* spoke to the commander of the Starfleet force and confirmed everything the Klingons had been saying."

"But that's impossible!" Kirk whispered, staring at her face with a mixture of fear and hope.

"I'll show you. Come on." She got to her feet, pulling him after her. "That was history class. Now you get to see a movie."

Kirk didn't understand, didn't respond to her banter. "It's all right, Jim!" she said urgently. "You'll see. It's the truth—and it all keeps getting better from here."

The wall screen before them glowed pink, and then a picture formed on it. Kirk caught his breath. He was looking down on the bridge of a Federation starship. Beneath him was the familiar layout, and familiar, too, were the figures on the bridge: Spock, Uhura, Sulu, Chekov . . .

"Old records," Kalrind explained, oblivious to Kirk's emotions. "The Federation passed copies on to us, and we combined them with some of our own. They've just heard your message of peace broadcast from the Klingon fleet. Listen."

Spock occupied the command seat. He thumbed a switch on the chair arm. "Analysis, Doctor?"

Leonard McCoy's voice sounded puzzled. "I don't know, Spock. My gut feeling is suspicion."

"Conclusion, Doctor?" Spock sounded impatient—a subtle hint in his voice that no one but Kirk could have detected.

"Since I'm a doctor and not a computer," McCoy said sarcastically, "unlike some people I could name but won't, I don't *have* any conclusions. That's for commander types, not for country doctors. My *inclination,* however, is not to believe it. Let's hold off for a while and see what he says next. After all, the more we hear, the more data we have to analyze."

Spock nodded. "Surprisingly logical, Doctor."

Kirk found himself grinning. *I don't need voice analysis to know that that exchange was for real,* he thought. *Poor Spock—he looks so worried, so worn out.* Kirk wanted to speak to his friend, to communicate with him somehow, and reassure him. A sudden awareness of the reality brought him up short. *That all happened a hundred years ago!* It brought it home all over again: everyone on that screen was dead, utterly lost to him.

The view shifted to the bridge of another Starfleet vessel, where a communication was received from *Enterprise* conveying McCoy's conclusion and Spock's concurrence in it. That was followed in turn by scenes on the bridges of Klingon ships in the fleet, where worried Klingon officers were shown discussing the chances that the Starfleet commanders would believe Kirk on the one hand, or open fire on the other.

When the screen finally went blank again, Kirk was surprised at how shaken and disoriented he felt.

"Okay," Kalrind said enthusiastically. "That was

the first day. Now I've got to try and find the next day's recordings."

"I'd like to see my own speech to them. Can you show me that?"

Kalrind shook her head. "Sorry, Jim. The records are incomplete, both ours and Starfleet's. A lot of our shipboard recordings were lost during the upheavals in the Empire that followed the Tholian Incident—when the New Klingons were taking over. Starfleet doesn't know why their recordings are incomplete, but they haven't been able to find everything in their archives. Inefficiency, maybe."

"Just barely possible," Kirk said with a smile.

"Anyway, it's a tragedy for historians, but your actual speech itself is lost. We've been able to reconstruct the words you spoke from these recordings, but we have no recording of you actually speaking them. Okay, now." She turned back to the keyboard and worked with it. "Here it is, I think."

On screen, Spock was in the *Enterprise* Sickbay talking to Leonard McCoy. "Doctor," he said, "we have ample data for analysis by now, and even though I have learned through long association with Captain Kirk to respect human intuition, I must lend greater weight to instrument analysis. I have therefore decided to accept the computer's conclusions and to recommend to the rest of the fleet that they do the same."

McCoy said angrily, "Damn it, Spock, what would Jim say?"

"Precisely, Doctor. We already know the answer to that question."

The next scene showed the Klingons smiling in relief as they were told that the officers commanding the vast array of Starfleet ships had voted to believe the message from Captain James Kirk. And so the Klingon fleet was escorted triumphantly all the way to Earth, where amid worldwide (later to become Federation-wide) celebrations the Great Peace was initiated.

The wall screen went blank again. "There you are!" Kalrind said triumphantly. "The Great Peace has lasted ever since then, a whole century! Neither side has breached it in all that time!"

Kirk realized that he had tears in his eyes—more from seeing his friends on the wall screen than from what Kalrind had just said. "Few of us hoped for that," he said.

"I know," Kalrind said comfortingly. "You know, Jim, the alliance between the Federation and the Empire has grown still closer during that century. There hasn't even been what you could call a border incident for something like seventy-five years. In fact, there's scarcely a frontier anymore. Klingons and Federationists travel unimpeded in each other's territories. A complete political union will probably come about in my lifetime. A *jIjmoS,* as we would say. And in time—who knows?—perhaps the Romulans will agree to join it, as well. No, not 'perhaps,' Jim: I'm *sure* they will."

Kirk felt distracted. "That's good," he said absently. "But this Tholian Incident and my part in it—why, it's impossible! I couldn't have been there, not in anyone's fleet. I was thrown forward in time *before* any of that happened!"

Kalrind smiled. "We know, Jim—and we think we know what really happened. I'd like to have Morith give you the next part of the explanation."

They found Morith in a laboratory workroom, sitting at a small table surrounded by unidentifiable equipment. He was typing on a keyboard integrated into the table, and he looked up with momentary annoyance at being interrupted. His face cleared when he saw who had interrupted him, and he smiled. "Jim! This is a pleasure." Then he glanced at Kalrind and back at Kirk again. "Aah. I see. Just a moment."

He typed some final instructions into the keyboard, stood up, and stretched. "What point have you reached?"

Kalrind said, "I've given him an outline of the Tholian Incident, and how it ended."

"She told me what she knew about it," Kirk added. "Which is apparently not all that much. She said the next information comes from you. So what *is* next?" Kirk was aware of feelings of animosity within himself: he was tired of all this mystery, tired of feeling under the control of others, tired of feeling that he was being shunted from one Klingon to another, with each one giving him only a tantalizing piece of the story he wanted to hear, before telling him that someone else would provide the next chapter.

Ignoring the undertone of hostility in Kirk's voice, Morith said, "What's next is the largest fleet of spacecraft in history. Would you like to see it?"

Kirk stared at him, too surprised to speak. Morith smiled. "Follow me."

They were in a room Kirk had never visited before. Kalrind had not accompanied them, though she would follow soon. "I shouldn't even be involved in this," Morith said. "I'm a physicist, a very theoretical scientist. I don't know who decided I should be given an administrative job like this."

"Technical planning," Kirk said absently, stepping forward toward the giant screen.

"Yes, that must be it." Morith nodded. "Someone on Klinzhai had the silly idea that since I *am* a physicist, I should be able to handle technical planning. Makes one wonder how our ancestors built such a large empire in the first place, doesn't it?''

''I don't think the Old Klingons suffered from that kind of confusion.'' *And yet they would have been at home with this fleet.*

One wall of the room was a screen much like those on the bridge of *Enterprise*. Morith had explained that although this screen had been intended for scientific use, it was the most convenient one to show Kirk what he wanted to show him. And now the far wall of the room had become an electronic window into space. It was as if the wall were of glass and there was nothing, no rock, no concrete, between Kirk and the vast emptiness and the great fleet that hung out there, orbiting the base.

Many of the ships were no more than lights winking against the many-colored stars, or small dark shapes that blocked those stars, silhouetted against them. Others were closer and were transfixed by powerful beams of light from the Klingon station. Those transfixed Kirk.

Klingon birds of prey. They bristled with armament, obvious to Kirk's practiced eye. ''Those are warships, Morith,'' he said. ''Klingon warships from my own time.''

The Klingon looked embarrassed. ''That's all that was available. It's a heritage from our past. A remnant of it, I should say. We couldn't afford to strip our trade, our mercantile fleet, for this mission, so they recommissioned and reconditioned all the old ships they could get their hands on. Those *are* warships left over from your own time, Jim. That's the last time Klingons built spaceships for war. We have them in museums all over the Empire, well maintained. We show them to our young to instill in them shame and fear of our past. But on the positive side, it meant that those old ships were available to make up the fleet for this mission when other ships weren't."

"And what *is* that mission?" Kirk asked again. He had asked the same question a few minutes earlier, and Morith had refused to answer him. Now, as before, Morith refused, and he gave the same reason: "Wait until Kalrind gets here. I'll answer you then." Only rarely had Morith struck Kirk as the sort of man who needed such moral support.

And so they waited in silence, each occupied with his own thoughts, alone in the small viewing room. Morith's attention seemed directed inward; Kirk's, inevitably, was drawn outward by the fleet—drawn into the void, into his proper realm.

At last Kirk heard Kalrind's distinctive footsteps hurrying down the hallway. As soon as she entered the room, he said, "Now, Morith. Please, no more delays."

Morith nodded. He walked over to the screen, next to Kirk, and stared into the blackness. "That fleet," he gestured, "will become the New Klingon fleet that confronts the Federation fleet near Tholia. Those ships and the three of us will travel in time one hundred years to play our proper roles in the Tholian Incident."

They were back in the laboratory workroom where Kirk and Kalrind had earlier found Morith. Morith had been quite right to wait for Kalrind, Kirk realized: Morith hadn't needed her support, but Kirk had. He was shaken by Morith's reference to time-travel plans, disoriented by it. He had held his peace while they walked back here, but now he was bursting with questions.

For a moment, though, he stared wordlessly at the two Klingons. After what had seemed an endless period of adjustment to his terrible loss, he could hardly believe that they were telling him that his world was not lost after all.

Morith began. "We have a plan, devised by our own Klingon scientists in cooperation with human experts in the Federation. They discussed it for quite some time, but now they agree about what we have to do. We must travel back in time ourselves to make sure you're there where and when you need to be. In other words, we have to make sure history happens correctly."

Kirk shook his head in amazement, but Kalrind took his gesture for disapproval. "It's really quite simple, Jim," she said. "In essence, anyway. You see, back then, the New Klingons were still struggling with the Old Klingons for control of the Empire. Why should we just let the outcome of that struggle be subject to the whims of history? We know it worked out the way we want, but what tipped the balance? What made it come out the way we wanted, instead of the other way?"

Kirk was confused. "Does it matter? It happened. That's what counts, not how close things came to going some other way."

"Yes, but it could change."

"The past could change? Nonsense. The past is over with." But then Kirk remembered New York in 1930 and the death of Edith Keeler. "It *can* be changed," he said softly. He shivered suddenly. "The past can be a terrible thing to meddle with."

"But not if you're meddling to make sure the results are good," Morith said urgently.

"Don't be so sure." Kirk had let Edith die on Earth

in 1930, precisely in order to make sure that the results were good, and that decision had haunted him ever since.

Kalrind went on, "We will send this armada back a hundred years so that it can be the New Klingon fleet and turn the Tholian Incident into the Great Peace. You'll be on the flagship, and so will I. What historian could miss such an opportunity?"

"You don't know how dangerous this is," Kirk told her.

"Not dangerous at all," Morith said brusquely. "We've worked out virtually every detail."

"Why the fleet?" Kirk asked him. "Why not just one or two ships?"

"And how do you think the Old Klingons of your time would react if they detected one or two ships headed for the frontier, Jim? The ships would be stopped. But the way the Old Klingons tended to think, they wouldn't dare to interfere with such a fleet. They'll assume that it must have been authorized. And by the time they find out the truth, it'll be too late. The Great Peace will be underway.

"Besides," Morith went on after a pause, "these ships were available immediately, and it would have taken time to obtain any others. And we don't have time. Time is pressing."

"Pressing!" Kirk exclaimed. "How can that be? We're going back to a chosen point in a previous time. That won't change. How can time be pressing for us now, a hundred years later?"

Morith grimaced. "I was putting off going into all of this, because I have trouble explaining it. I believe you traveled into the past yourself, by using the gravitational field of a star?"

"Yes, that's true," Kirk said, amazed. "But how

did you know that? That's secret Starfleet information!"

Morith laughed. "*Was* secret, Jim, *was* secret! Everything in Federation records is available to us now, and the reverse is also true. That mission was one of the famous adventures of the great Captain Kirk. It's one of the stories our schoolchildren are reared on!"

Kirk gestured, a motion of futility. "I'm not sure I'll ever get used to this—this new perspective."

"You won't need to if this mission succeeds. As I was about to say, we're going to use a very similar technique to go back a hundred years. Our physicists have only recently discovered a supermassive body not far from our frontier with the Federation, in the direction of Tholia. It's one member of a binary pair, the other member being a white dwarf star. You used the field of an ordinary star, but this body will give us better control, and it will enable us to translate this entire fleet back in time. Back a hundred years."

"I've never heard of such a body in that area."

"No. It was discovered quite recently. We call it *Hov tInqu'*."

"Which means?"

Morith laughed. "In English, roughly something like, um, 'very big star.' Now, you see, the reason time is important is that where—when, I mean—we end up in the past is a complicated function of the time when we enter *Hov tInqu's* gravitational field, as well as the angle and speed of entry. Moreover, the function is quantized. By that I mean that only certain times in the past are accessible, because only certain combinations of time, angle, and speed will work. In fact, it will be a very dangerous trip for the fleet, because a minute error in time or angle or speed will result in destruction by the powerful gravitational field, instead of transfer in time. One way, you jump in time; any other, and you're crushed."

Kirk nodded. He knew that much about this method of time travel, at least.

"We've calculated it over and over in order to be absolutely sure, and we keep coming up with the same answer. *Hov tInqu'* will allow us to jump back to just the right time, the moment before the Tholian Incident began. That's remarkable luck, Jim, but there's only one combination of time, angle of entry, and speed of entry that will get us there, and that time is coming up very soon. It's only days away. We—the fleet, I mean—will have to leave this base within twenty hours at the very most."

Chapter Nine

FLEET ADMIRAL CHUNG prided himself on his impassivity, which he considered the equal of any Vulcan's, but today his face betrayed equal mixtures of annoyance and puzzlement as Spock entered his office.

Spock saluted and stood at attention before the admiral's desk. "Well, Mr. Spock?" Chung said testily. "Now what? You requested that we allow you to file your report by hyperspace radio rather than being required to report directly back here which, after a great deal of internal discussion, we agreed to do—and yet now you show up in San Francisco! We have long made special allowances for you and Captain Kirk. You've both been granted quite a few privileges, compared to other officers in the fleet."

As Chung lectured on, Spock stood at attention with his face expressionless—unintentionally serving as a model of that emotionless appearance to which the admiral aspired. This only served to increase Chung's anger. "You've both deserved special treatment," Chung continued, "because of your brilliant records. But now, Spock, this time—" He paused for a breath. The longer he ranted at Spock, the longer the Vulcan stood there absolutely calm. Chung felt his temper escaping his control. "This time, Spock, you've overdone it! A starship captain disappears, and yet despite that, I give you permission to stay at Starbase Seventeen—and the next thing I know you show up here in San Francisco! Well?"

"Well what, Admiral?" Spock asked.

Chung pounded a fist against his desk. "I ought to—! Don't try to—! SPOCK!"

Spock said patiently, "I'm sorry, Admiral, but I don't understand what it is you want to know. If you would be so kind as to explain."

Retirement, Chung thought. *Only a year to go*. "I want to know," Chung said tightly, "what you are doing here."

"Ah," Spock said. "Now I understand. Thank you, Admiral."

Chung took a deep breath and squeezed his eyes shut for a moment. He opened them. "Continue, Mr. Spock," he said resignedly.

"I would have sent you a message in advance, Admiral, to explain my visit here, but I had reason to fear interception of my message."

The admiral sat back in his chair. "What are you telling me, Spock?"

"I needed your permission, sir, to perform some experiments using a piece of top-secret equipment kept here at Starfleet Headquarters. Since Starfleet has tried to keep secret even the existence of that piece of hardware, let alone its location, I thought it wisest to make the request in person. Moreover, when you grant the request, I will need to be here anyway to perform the experiments I have in mind."

" '*When*,' Spock, not '*if*' I grant your request?" Chung shook his head. "All right, Spock, just what is it that you're requesting? What piece of top-secret hardware do you need?"

Spock told him.

Chung stared for a long time. Then he said, "Permission granted. Wait a minute. Are you sure? Never mind. Stupid question. Vulcans are always sure."

"I believe that's a fair assessment, Admiral," Spock said, taking the remark at face value.

Chung grimaced. "Anything else?"

"I could use some assistance, sir. It would speed matters up."

"Of course," Chung added. "Let's see, I'll give Admiral Kim a call—"

"I did have someone in mind." Spock interrupted. "Elliot Tindall."

Naturally, Chung thought to himself. But Tindall's a good man, so—"What's the date?" He looked at his desk calendar. "Oh, yes. I believe he returned from his vacation this morning. Let me give him a call." He reached for the communicator on his desk.

"Admiral," Spock said quickly, "I'd prefer it if you didn't do that. No communications net can ever be entirely secure. Could we visit him at home instead?"

"Hmph. Spock, do you really think Starfleet communications can be compromised?"

"*Any* communications net can be, Admiral," Spock said.

"Oh, all right. I'll call for a driver. You will allow that, I suppose?" Chung said with heavy sarcasm.

Spock considered the question for a moment. "Yes, Admiral. Please feel free."

"Why, thank you, Mr. Spock." Chung emphasized the rank, but of course sarcasm was always lost on Spock—at least, so far as any human could tell.

* * *

Arguments had become increasingly common at the Tindall home. Usually, though, they managed to keep the arguments quiet—at least, quiet enough that the neighbors didn't hear. Today, though, Elliot and Luisa were being loud enough for the neighbors and the two uniformed visitors coming up the front walk to hear. The neighbors listened raptly from behind curtains. The two visitors had no choice but to pretend to ignore what they heard.

Luisa answered the door. Chung noticed the redness of her eyes and nose. "Oh, Admiral," Luisa said. "Hello. Come in. Elliot's in his study. I'll go get him."

"I'm sorry to have to disturb you while he's still on vacation, Luisa," Chung said awkwardly, "but this is very important."

Luisa smiled tightly and said nothing. She led them down a short hallway to a living room furnished in the softly padded furniture that had become fashionable on Earth lately. The prints on the wall and the pale color scheme all fit in with the latest style among Earth's upper middle classes.

"Please," Luisa said, pointing at the couch. She left the room, audibly muffling a sob.

Spock and Chung sat down side by side on the couch, the Vulcan showing no awkwardness at all, while Chung felt both uncomfortable and unhappy. They ignored each other, Chung choosing to examine the prints on the wall rather than make eye contact with his companion.

After a while heavy footsteps came down the hallway toward them, and Elliot Tindall strode into the room and stopped. "Admiral Chung," he said, staring with easily detected hostility, "I don't think I'm due in the office until next Monday. Or did I miscalculate?"

"Oh, no, Elliot, not at all," Chung said with exaggerated heartiness. "You're quite right. Unfortunately, though, something quite urgent has come up. I don't know if you've ever met Mr. Spock . . .?"

Elliot turned his attention to the Vulcan, who had risen to his feet and stood waiting silently. "No, but of course I know of you, sir. Probably the most famous Vulcan in Starfleet." He smiled to make it clear he was joking.

Spock took the remark seriously. "I have little competition for that distinction, Mr. Tindall."

"And I've always thought that was a shame, sir," Elliot said quickly. "The Science Division could use the Vulcan approach to technical problems. I have, for example, long admired the writings of Meng."

Spock nodded. "One of our finest philosophers of science. And I have heard of you, Mr. Tindall. I've read your paper on the interaction of the T-jump effect and the transporter phase field and found it closely reasoned and admirably concise."

Chung watched the interplay between the two. Convinced that it was as amiable as it sounded, he relaxed. "Elliot, Mr. Spock has come to Earth to do some very important work. He has requested you as his assistant."

"Why, I'd be honored!" Elliot broke in. "It would be a wonderful opportunity!"

"Yes, I realize that," Chung continued. "But it would mean you'd have to temporarily abandon your current project."

"Nothing," Elliot said immediately. "No problem at all. If Mr. Spock needs my help, nothing else stands in the way."

"Perhaps you'd like to know what my needs are," Spock said.

"Whatever they are, sir, I'd be honored to participate."

"Immediately?" Chung asked. "Today? Right now?"

Elliot shrugged. "If it's that urgent, Admiral, of course."

"You can tell Luisa it's all my fault," Chung began in a jovial tone and then kicked himself mentally as soon as the words were out.

Elliot's posture grew stiff and cold in a subtle but unmistakable fashion. "I'll manage that problem, Admiral."

Chung sprang to his feet. "Well! Now that that's all settled," he said, "we need to be on our way—all of us. Mr. Spock and I will wait for you outside, Elliot, while you . . . um."

Elliot nodded. "I'll be with you in a few minutes."

Chung led the way quickly out of the house and into their waiting vehicle. Once they were safely inside, insulated from their driver's hearing, he said, "I don't understand it, Mr. Spock, I just don't understand it. They were always so happy. What's gone wrong?" He sighed. "I don't know what's wrong with the young these days. It was different in my day. Everything they do seems so impermanent. They lack commitment. I'm beginning to worry seriously about the future of the human race."

Spock said, "Admiral, you are echoing the complaint of many a philosopher of previous times. It seems to be a peculiarly human failing to see one's own age as a pale and inferior stepchild of all previous ages. What humans lack, I think, is an objective and unemotional view of their history."

Chung expected him to expound on this topic at much greater length, but then Elliot Tindall walked out of his house to join them.

Days of intensive work followed.

Spock and Elliot worked long hours and took only short breaks. Elliot almost matched the Vulcan in his ability to ignore the need for food and sleep. They both outlasted the small team of assistants that had been assigned to them; in the end the two of them did the great bulk of the work.

The theory underlying the hardware Spock had requisitioned had to be extended and more deeply understood before the testing of Spock's hypothesis could even begin, and major modifications to the hardware had to be worked out as well. In both tasks, Elliot's contribution was a significant factor in their final success.

When the tests finally got under way, the two of them were alone in the workshop Starfleet had assigned to them. Their three assistants were all asleep, trying to recover from the last unending bout during which Spock and Elliot, in a long burst, had completed the final stage of the work.

It was more than dedication to the work and fascination with it and the opportunity to work with Spock that had kept Elliot in the workshop for such long hours. It was also his spending the last two days of their sustained push sleeping at the base instead of home. The relationship with Luisa had reached a point at which he no longer trusted himself alone with her. The thought that he might, in uncontrolled anger, harm her, perhaps even kill her, terrified him.

Elliot remembered first meeting Luisa and their first year together. Happy as he knew she had been, he had been even happier. It was the medication that had made even that possible. But now that he had reached what should have been the fulfillment of his assigned duties and the completion of his personal happiness, his medication was betraying him.

In fact, he was badly overdue for his dose. Uncharacteristically hasty and distracted, he had left the bottle of pills at home. How could he get it without encountering Luisa (and all the tears and pleading and inevitable fury that would result)? He was supposed to take the pills daily and had been warned of awful things if he failed to do so. He had already missed his regular dose twice. He hoped that, after taking the medication for so many years, he had built up enough of it in his blood that he could manage to miss a few days without dangerous results.

"Mr. Tindall," Spock said sharply, "I requested an increase in power."

Elliot snapped back to an awareness of his surroundings and duties. "Oh, yes, Yes, of course. Sorry, Mr. Spock. I was daydreaming." He turned the dial quickly, boosting power by the amount Spock's experimental schedule required.

Spock turned back to his monitor, saying nothing about the human propensity for daydreaming, as contrasted to the Vulcan ability to ignore all distractions and discipline all thoughts, but he didn't need to. Elliot ascribed such opinions to him even without any words. *Damned supercilious Vulcan!* Elliot thought. *I'd like to*—Angrily, he squelched that thought. A bit of Vulcan mental discipline would be useful right now.

"How does it look, Mr. Spock?" he called out cheerfully.

Spock twisted around and looked at him in surprise, then returned to his study of the graph on the monitor.

"Following predictions so far, Mr. Tindall. Keep increasing the power according to the schedule."

I could sabotage his test so easily, Elliot thought suddenly. *That might be the best thing*. But no: Spock would notice immediately.

The process continued for more than two hours. By the time they reached the end of the planned test run, Elliot was feeling the strain—both the physical strain of concentrating and following the schedule, and the psychological strain of keeping his ever more unruly temper under control.

At last Spock stood up and said thoughtfully, "You may power down now, Mr. Tindall. I believe I have determined what I set out to."

Elliot rose, too, his nerves tingling. His muscles were stiff, but tensed for action. "So what's the next step?" he asked in a calm tone.

Spock stared at the young scientist for a moment as if measuring him in some way, weighing him. "My results mandate an immediate return to Starbase Seventeen. I've thought of requesting that you be assigned to accompany me. I've been very impressed with your work, and I believe you could contribute significantly in the next step. There would be danger; it would be very different from intellectual work here on Earth."

Elliot relaxed. This was far better than the action he had been planning! "I would be honored and delighted, Mr. Spock."

Spock nodded as if he had expected no other response. "Good. I will speak to Fleet Admiral Chung right away."

"How many days before we leave?"

"Not days, Mr. Tindall: minutes, if immediate transportation is available. Hours, otherwise. Starfleet has accorded my mission the highest possible priority."

Elliot gritted his teeth. He noticed Spock staring curiously at his bunching jaw muscles and forced himself to relax. "I'll be ready, Mr. Spock. I'll need to make a quick trip home, but I'll be ready."

Maybe it was working already, Luisa thought, working in some magical way. Then she felt ashamed of herself for thinking such a superstitious thought. Still, her friend had assured her that the supplements had worked wonders with her own husband, who had become a tyrant but was now as gentle and loving as in the early days of their marriage. How dearly Luisa wanted to recapture that same mood with Elliot!

And it was undeniable that during his few minutes at home, rushed as he was, he had been more like his old self. Of course she knew that the pills she had substituted for those worthless vitamins of his could hardly have worked on him while they were still in the bottle, but she wanted so much for them to work. She needed the old Elliot for her own survival.

It was remarkable good fortune that the supplements her friend had given her looked just like Elliot's vitamins. It was also fortunate that he had called her from the base before coming home, giving her just the time she needed. And finally, it was fortunate that he *had* been so rushed, or he might have noticed the pile of small, red capsules in the trash can in the bathroom, for Luisa had not had time to dispose of his vitamin pills properly. If he had noticed the pills and discovered what she had done, which Elliot would he have been?

She had felt desperate enough to resort to this subterfuge, this trickery, because the alternative—leaving Elliot—was too awful to think about.

Don't start thinking gloomy thoughts again, she ordered herself. *Wherever it is he's gone, he'll come back acting like the Elliot you fell in love with.*

Chapter Ten

DURING THE TRIP from the base to the supermassive body, Kirk continually interfered with Kalrind's work, oblivious to her occasional annoyance; there were still questions he wanted answered.

"How do we know that this scheme of yours is really the way it happened?" he persisted in asking. "There must be records. Your own records, or maybe Federation records; they'd show us *how* I got there, how I managed to be present at the Tholian Incident. So we'd know if we're doing the right thing." *God knows*, he told himself grimly, *when you're traveling in the past, you don't want to do the wrong one.* "Starfleet must have debriefed me after it was all over."

"You would think so," Kalrind agreed. "However, Federation personnel have searched their archives without finding any records of such a debriefing. Actually, in retrospect, it doesn't seem that surprising. Just imagine how everyone must have felt, on both sides—the jubilation, the celebrations, the . . . the *delight*! Who worried about debriefing and other formalities like that?"

She laughed suddenly. "And one thing I haven't

even told you! As soon as the Great Peace was announced, Admiral James T. Kirk resigned his commission and was appointed the Federation's first ambassador to the Klingon Empire. That, by the way, was at the request of the commanders of both fleets, both the Federation and Klingon fleets. Everyone who had been involved in the Tholian Incident was impressed by his diplomacy."

"Ambassdor to the Klingon Empire?" Kirk said wonderingly. "What an amazing idea!"

Kalrind, unusually coy, said, "You know, when you were assigned to the Empire, you probably romanced my great-great-great-grandmother. From what I've heard, it's not the sort of thing she would have told anyone. I may be your descendant."

Kirk stared at her, more disturbed at the possibility than he was willing to tell her. Kalrind laughed at his expression. "But probably not. Don't worry about it. You'll probably have your choice of Klingon women. We all like the exotic, the different, and humans are as exotic and different as they come. I bet women in the Federation are like that just as much as those in the Empire."

Kirk opened his mouth, but then shut it without saying anything.

"Now," she continued, "on to more practical matters. I need some specific information from you, Jim. Or I should say, *we* need it. We need it to make sure history remains unchanged. As you said, we need to make sure we're doing everything correctly."

There was, Kirk thought, one way in which the New Klingons were certainly very different from the Old: the Old Klingons were blunt and direct, while the New were circumlocutory. In this respect, Kirk found he preferred the older version of the breed. At first, he had been overwhelmed by the idea of regaining the world—the time—he had thought lost. Now he began to fear losing Kalrind even more. Changing the past, he feared, would tear her from him just as it had torn Edith Keeler from him. But when he tried to move their conversations in that direction, in the direction of possible dangers to their relationship from this undertaking, Kalrind always retreated behind a barrier of professional investigation: she became the historian, and he became her source; their status as lovers became a subject not to be discussed.

And when he complained openly about this, she said, "Please, Jim. Be patient. All of this is very bizarre, very amazing—both what we're all trying to do and what's happened between the two of us. I need your famous tolerance."

"I'm famous for being *tolerant?*" Kirk shook his head. "That gives me an entirely new perspective on history. I'm going to have to change my opinion of a whole lot of historical characters." He reached out and stroked Kalrind's hair. "But I'll try."

"I just thought of something!" Kalrind said suddenly. "Now, what was it? Oh, yes, that's right. I can't think when you touch me!" She moved away from him. "See: now my memory returns immediately. You humans . . . ! I just realized that I'll be there, too, so you won't get the chance to romance my ancestress, after all! I'll be with you instead, when you become the Federation ambassador to the Klingon Empire."

He would return to his own time and live a long and peaceful and productive life with Kalrind by his side! Kirk was astonished at the strength of the longing that consumed him, the longing she had painted so simply and easily and with so few words. It overwhelmed his fear.

"Right on schedule," Morith said happily.

Before them, on the screen that formed the forward wall of the *Alliance* bridge, was the achingly familiar starfield. Being on the bridge of a ship, watching the stars crawling off to the side of the screen, Kirk felt almost at home again, although he knew he wouldn't feel fully secure until he was on the bridge of a Federation starship and back in his own time. If Morith and his fellow scientists were right, all of that would happen very soon.

In the middle of the starfield, a dim, hazy blue sphere glowed faintly. This was the supermassive body of which Morith had told him: their gateway into the past.

"We're actually seeing certain levels of its gravitational field," Morith explained. "The light is given off by the constant destruction of infalling stellar matter from the body's companion star, which is invisible to us. Of the particles falling into the supermassive body, some transfer to other times, but most are destroyed, instantaneously turned to energy."

As we could be, Kirk thought.

"And us, Morith?" Kalrind asked, echoing his thoughts. "Could we be destroyed too? Converted to energy?"

In answer, Morith continued his explanation. "As I told you before, time transition takes place only at certain critical, quantized combinations of time, angle, and speed of entry. Of course, most particles don't happen to hit such a combination, and those are converted to energy. At what radius that happens also depends on time and angle and speed of entry. That's why I said we're seeing different levels of its gravitational field."

The different levels at which we could flash into heat and light if we're off in any one of the critical parameters, Kirk thought. And if they were off but managed to hit another critical combination, would they end up at some other point in the past? He had neglected to ask Morith that. Would they end up in 1930, perhaps?

Time travel, if it were controllable, offered so many ways to change the past. Too many ways. That was why it could not be used, why a wise society avoided or even outlawed it. *But this time, how could the goal be nobler*?

Kirk turned around slowly, looking not at the crowded bridge of the Klingon ship, but at the screens, which showed the space around the ship. To the sides and behind them, above and below, blinking lights showed the location of the other members of the enormous fleet of which *Alliance* was the flagship.

The hours passed, the glowing body swelling in the forward viewscreen, becoming both larger and solider, its brightness increasing as it grew into something real and immense and overwhelming.

Kirk and Kalrind spent those hours on the bridge with Morith, crowded together on the small, fenced dais upon which the control seat was placed, looking down on the quiet, busy, efficient Klingons manning the various posts controlling the ship. To Kirk's eye, the posts had not been modified from their original functions of a hundred years ago, but he knew from what he had seen of the Klingons' technological advances that the circuitry behind the panels was entirely different. Examining the bridge crew and trying to interpret their actions by analogy to those of the crew on the bridge of the ship he knew so well, his own ship, killed the time and took Kirk's mind from their impending and dangerous passage.

The tension on the bridge grew steadily. Even though these people were of another species and their body language was subtly but essentially different, Kirk could sense their growing nervousness. Kalrind pressed closer against his side. Only Morith seemed calm.

"Are you sure," Kirk asked him in a low voice so that none of the crew would hear him, "that the navigation is precise enough?"

Morith smiled at him. "Don't worry about it, Jim. History says you were there, at the Tholian Incident. Therefore, I know you *will* be."

Kalrind must not have been quite so convinced by recorded history, despite her long study of it. She gripped Kirk's arm painfully and leaned against him. He could feel that she was trembling.

As Kirk watched her, filled with concern and love for her, her face was bathed in a blue glow. No, it wasn't just Kalrind: it was everything. The light was coming from the screen. Someone on the bridge moaned, a low, long sound of fear.

On the forward screen, the supermassive body had blotted out the stars. Even in the corners of the rectangular screen, not covered by the body, the fierce blue glare of dying stellar matter made the stars invisible. The glow was steady, unflickering, not a candle to light the darkness but a monstrous anomaly swallowing the light of its neighboring star.

Alliance trembled, shuddered throughout its entire mass. Kirk felt a moment of sickness and disorientation. Weakness overcame him, and he would have fallen but for Kalrind's strong arm bearing him up.

And then the glow was gone, and only the beauty of star-filled space lay ahead of them.

Morith said calmly, "Obviously we transited successfully." He said something in Klingon to one of the figures hunched over a monitor on the bridge's lower level. The man answered in Klingon, and Morith sighed. He said sadly to Kirk, "And so did all but one vessel of our fleet."

Kirk hardly heard him. He was home.

The mood onboard ship changed drastically. Where before the Klingon crew had behaved as if they were facing execution, now they acted like a crew on holiday. They were on their way into history; they were creating the *Roj tIn*.

Kirk and Kalrind were able to spend time with each other again, as they had not been able to during the last few days. Kirk had found the constant presence of others during the day annoying; on the base, he had grown used to being alone with Kalrind and spending hours simply talking to her—with him talking and her listening, as she seemed to prefer. He had noticed during the last day or so that even Kalrind, normally so placid and amiable, had been growing short-tempered at their situation. She had occasionally snapped at him, and even though she would apologize profusely afterward, Kirk felt it would be best if they could be alone together as soon as possible in order to reclaim their past happiness—the combination of comradeship and tenderness that had become so important to him so quickly.

Partly it was the excitement and tension and bustle connected with approaching and then passing through the supermassive body that had interfered with them. But they had also been hampered by the ship itself.

Alliance was large for a Klingon ship, but it was still far smaller than the base had been. Relatively, it was more densely populated. There seemed to be few places for them to wander unobserved and uninterrupted.

"So we'll find someplace," Kirk said. "Let's go roaming."

"I'm not sure we ought to," Kalrind said reluctantly.

"You enjoyed doing that with me on the base," Kirk pointed out. "Look, we can't contribute anything, anyway. You're an historian, and I'm an outdated space sailor who grew up with ancient hardware. We're just in the way now. Come on." He took her arm.

"All right!" Kalrind jerked her arm away from him. "Don't touch me. I don't . . . feel like being touched."

Kirk shrugged and led the way down the nearest hallway, turning his face away so that she wouldn't see how hurt he was.

At first, she stayed behind him, deliberately avoiding catching up, but as they traveled through the ship, Kalrind's better nature seemed to take control again. She moved up beside Kirk and linked arms with him.

"Sorry," she said, smiling.

Finally, they found themselves in a short hallway in which they could not see or hear anyone else.

They grinned at each other. "What's that word you use?" Kalrind asked, her good humor quite restored "Bingo?"

Kirk laughed. "That's the one. Learned it from my grandmother."

Then they turned the corner at the end of the corridor.

Facing them was a heavy metal door, flanked by two

enormous, grim-faced guards. Each of them held a phaser rifle, unchanged from the Klingon weapons of that type from Kirk's days. Kirk could see in their faces none of the amiability he had learned to expect from New Klingons. These two might have come from his own era.

Kalrind squeezed his arm, a signal, Kirk presumed, that he should hold back, but instead he stepped up to the two glowering Klingons and said jovially, "Gentlemen! Good day to you! Please open that door for us."

One of the guards snarled and said in heavily accented English, "Get away, Earther! Not go in here!"

Kirk held both hands up, palms out, clearly empty, and said in as friendly a tone as he could manage, "I don't think your attitude is proper, young man. I'm curious about what—"

At that moment, the guard who had spoken stepped forward threateningly, raised his weapon, and pointed it at Kirk.

"*yImev!*" It was Kalrind's voice, but with a power of command that Kirk had never heard from her before. Obediently, the guard stopped.

In English, Kalrind added, "Back to your post. We will leave." She took Kirk's arm and pulled him forcefully after her.

After they had turned the corner and were again in the isolated short corridor, Kirk said mildly, "Well, that was all quite unexpected."

"Yes," Kalrind said curtly. They walked in silence for a few minutes, and then she said, "Perhaps we should restrict our exploring."

"Hmm. Let's go find Morith."

The scientist was still on the bridge.

When Kirk and Kalrind told him about their encounter, he looked embarrassed. "The Romulans, Jim," he said.

"Yes? What about them?"

"You see, we're at peace with the Federation, but we're not at peace with the Roms, and neither are your people. We both have to keep some of the old ways alive to guard against them."

"Do you mean," Kirk asked in amazement, "that you're afraid they'll infiltrate your ships?"

"They have in the past. Disguised as Klingons, moreover."

"Surgery?"

"And drugs, to make their behavior appropriate."

It provided Kirk with much food for thought, but all of that fled his mind the next morning.

He awoke early. Sleepily, he turned toward Kalrind and shook her. She did not move.

Alarmed, Kirk sat up in bed and with a voice command turned on the overhead lights. Kalrind lay upon her back, eyes squeezed shut, face pale, trembling visibly. Beads of sweat stood upon her dark forehead.

Why, she's having a nightmare, Kirk thought. He put his hand on her shoulder and shook her, first gently, and then with increasing violence. It had no effect.

"Kalrind!" he said. There was desperation in his voice. *"Kalrind!"*

He yelled and shook her, imploring her to wake up. Finally, he leapt out of bed and hit the emergency button set in the wall—the same one Kalrind had used once before to summon help for him.

Morith was with the team that showed up in response to the alarm signal. He took one look at Kalrind and uttered a Klingon curse. He signaled to the emergency team and then turned to Kirk.

"Jim! She'll be all right. Don't worry!"

Kirk watched helplessly as the emergency team slid Kalrind onto a stretcher and rushed her from the room.

Chapter Eleven

"I ASSURE YOU, JIM," Morith repeated patiently. "She will be all right."

"But I just don't understand! What could have happened?"

Morith hesitated and then said, "Have you ever heard of the *Qong-Hegh?*"

Kirk repeated the word, fumbling with the Klingon consonants. "No."

They were in Morith's cramped office just off the bridge, and Kirk was sitting in a chair in front of the desk, Morith behind it.

"Not surprising. It's something we don't discuss with non-Klingons—or with each other, for that matter. I suppose the best translation would be 'sleep death.' It's a hereditary disease that has been around since before our recorded history began. It's rare, and it used to be inevitably fatal."

Kirk jumped to his feet.

Morith held up a hand to forestall him. "*Used* to be, I said. We can control it with drugs, nowadays. Haven't you noticed Kalrind taking pills every day?"

Kirk thought about it. "Why, yes, I have. I asked her about it once, and she said it was some sort of vitamin supplement because of a metabolic problem she had inherited."

Morith laughed. "Not that far off the truth, except that what she inherited was a fatal disease, not a metabolic problem, and the pill isn't a vitamin supplement but rather the medication that keeps her alive."

"But why did she lie to me?"

"As I said, we don't discuss it. We're ashamed of it," Morith amplified. "It was always associated with the lowest classes in the old Empire, and even though we New Klingons profess not to care about any of that old social structure, there's still a great deal of shame attendant upon proof that one's ancestors were members of those classes. Inheriting *Qong-Hegh* is virtual proof of such descent."

Kirk shook his head. "It's foolish of her to be ashamed!"

With a rare flash of anger, Morith said harshly, "It's easy for an Earther to think so! You are not a product of our history, our warrior tradition. You can't understand how we feel!"

Kirk looked at him in mute surprise.

"Forgive me, Jim. The stress of running this fleet . . . It's not at all the work I was trained for.

"Anyway, to continue. In the old days, a child who displayed signs of the *Qong-Hegh* was simply allowed to die of it. That usually happened during adolescence, which is when the disease normally first manifests itself. Not that much could have been done even if anyone had wanted to save those children. It wasn't until the New Klingon takeover of the Empire that the situation changed, and that was only possible because of our breakthroughs in chemistry and biology, which together enabled us to design a drug therapy."

"But the breakthroughs came because the New

Klingons chose to direct their research in that direction," Kirk said thoughtfully.

Morith nodded. "A good point. Be that as it may, however, our immediate problem is Kalrind. The doctors report that her response to the drug is still normal. At first, they feared that it was losing its effect with her. That would be the first such case. However, she's returning to normal quickly with a course of treatment with the drug, fed intravenously in high doses, and they also determined before they began this treatment that the level of it in her blood was low. In other words, she had been neglecting to take her pill as required." He smiled. "Thanks to you, she had other things on her mind. Perhaps you noticed some slight personality change?"

"Not so slight," Kirk said. "She was becoming short-tempered, brusque."

"Yes. Typical symptoms, I'm told. From now on, Jim, I'd like you to assume the responsibility for Kalrind's health. We simply cannot do without her."

"Neither can I," Kirk said softly, and though he had spoken unconsciously, it was one of the truest things he had ever said.

"I understand," Morith said soothingly. "I'm asking you to see that she never again misses her daily dose. Her life depends on it. You can go to Sickbay now to see her, if you wish."

Kirk left, shaken, and made his way to *Alliance*'s Sickbay, so lost in thought that he did not notice the Klingons who passed him along the way and greeted him.

He found Kalrind sitting up in bed, her thick hair stringy with dried sweat, her face frighteningly pale. The only time he had ever seen a pale Klingon before was after that Klingon died.

He sat carefully on the side of her bed, afraid to shake it. "Have you been properly lectured?" he asked her. His tone was bantering, but beneath it lay a fear for her well-being which was so strong that it rendered him almost paralyzed.

Kalrind nodded. She reached for his hand and squeezed it, and Kirk was dismayed at the weakness he felt where he was used to feeling such strength. "Follow the rules," she said, her voice husky and weak. "Take my medication. You—you know about it?" There was fear in her voice.

Kirk nodded. "You don't have to pretend anymore. Morith explained all about it—the hereditary disease, the pills."

"Aah." Kalrind nodded. "Yes, I'm glad that he told you." Her eyelids drooped until her eyes were only half open. "I'm sorry, Jim. I'm worn out . . ."

Kirk stood up hastily. "No, *I'm* sorry. I shouldn't be bothering you while you're ill." He leaned over, kissed her forehead, and left the room. He strode rapidly, nervously down the main corridor on this level of the ship. *Exploration,* he told himself. *Absorb yourself in it.* Brooding about Kalrind's condition, her evident weakness, would be the most foolish thing he could do.

Instead, he headed for the nearest turbolift and took it up two floors, where he walked briskly toward the interesting corridor he and Kalrind had found before—the place where Old Klingon–style guards prevented access to a doorway.

Kirk was walking down the corridor, senses all alert, waiting for the first sign of the two massive guards, when a blazingly bright light floated around the next corner and confronted him. "Captain Kirk," the light greeted him. "Good day."

Kirk stopped in amazement. "What! Another Organian? I thought you people didn't want to have anything to do with us—either with the Federation or the Klingons. I seem to remember that when you imposed your treaty on us and the Klingons, you wrote something into it stating that neither power could even visit your world. If we can't visit Organia, and neither can the Klingons, why would you wish to visit us?"

The brilliant ball of light suspended in the air just above Kirk's head level, said, "I would stay to answer your questions, Captain, but I must hurry." He glided by the human.

"Wait!" Kirk said quickly. "Which Organian are you?"

"I am Ayleborne, whom you have met before."

"Yes, I have. You haven't answered my questions, Ayleborne."

An impatient voice came from the glowing light. "I have little time for this conversation, Kirk. I must be there when humans and New Klingons meet each other. Say what you want to, and then I must go."

"It seems to me," Kirk said, "that you would have an easier time getting both Klingons and Federationists to deal with you if you assumed material form—the way all of you did when we first encountered you. At that time, we thought you were humanoids, just like us. It does make communication easier."

The Organian did not deign to reply. *I suppose I'm too low an evolutionary level to understand the workings of an Organian mind,* Kirk thought with some annoyance.

Ayleborne floated down the hallway and turned a corner. As soon as he had done so, his light vanished, blinked out. Kirk ran down the hallway and around the corner, but it was deserted. It was as if the Organian had never been.

Kirk abandoned his exploration and returned to Morith's office.

Morith looked up when he entered. The Klingon's face betrayed a momentary annoyance, quickly masked. *He's busy and he'll probably consider this a trivial reason for an interruption,* Kirk thought guiltily. "I just ran into an Organian. Met him on the base, too. Not a very communicative fellow."

"Ah, yes. Ayleborne. As I understand it, he's something along the lines of a historian—although I'm sure that is an inadequate word for it. Perhaps beings such as Klingons and humans will never be able to understand Organians well enough to comprehend their social roles and divisions."

"What's he doing on *Alliance?*"

"Visting perhaps. Observing, more likely. He told me he's preoccupied with preparing for the historic meeting between Federationists and New Klingons. This is history, Jim, very important history! He's serving both as a scholar and as a representative of his race, watching the beginning of the alliance the Organians predicted would come about. You remember that prediction?"

Kirk nodded. "I'd be unlikely to forget it. But he's much less of a conversationalist than he was when I first met him."

"Hmm," Morith said thoughtfully. "I've always found him most polite. But not very forthcoming with information—you're right about that. All I know is that we were contacted by the Organians and told to take Ayleborne aboard. They seemed to know what we were planning even when we were still at the stage of discussing it only among ourselves."

"A breakdown in security. Heads have rolled for less."

Morith smiled—but it was the smile of a Klingon of old, not the transfiguring beautification of a New Klingon smile. "Whose head would you choose, Jim?"

Kirk turned aside. "Perhaps times have changed," he mumbled. In a louder voice, he said, "What have you heard about Kalrind?"

"Aah! The doctors say she is ready to be released. They pumped her full of the drug, and now she's back to normal. Do you mean you didn't visit her in Sickbay during her recuperation? Is that why you have to ask me about her condition?"

Kirk took in a deep breath and let it out. *For a theoretical physicist, he's one tough son-of-a-gun.* "I was there earlier. Briefly. I didn't want to go back immediately until I heard something definite, so I've been . . . waiting."

"You've been avoiding Sickbay because you feel guilty about Kalrind's illness, correct?"

"You learned this insight into human nature in one of your quantum mechanics classes, right?"

Morith laughed. "Observation, Jim. The basic training of every physicist—of every scientist. Go down to Sickbay and see your . . . friend."

As he left the office, Kirk reflected that Morith excelled him as an advanced master of the precisely calculated elliptical pause.

But then he reached Sickbay and forgot all of that in his delight at Kalrind's appearance.

To a Klingon, she would have appeared pale and weak, but to Kirk she seemed strong and vibrant—especially in contrast with a short time before. He embraced her. "You're all right!"

Kalrind smiled up at him. "Not entirely, but I'll

survive. Let's get me out of here." She turned to the communications unit beside her bed and said, "I want my doctor!" Kirk was encouraged by the strength and command in her voice.

A tinny voice responded. "This is Dr. Cherek, *joh* Kalrind. How may I serve?"

"Release me from this vile imprisonment, churl!" She winked at Kirk.

"Immediately. It is done. You may leave whenever you wish."

She turned he attention to Kirk. "A bit of traditional Klingon obedience has its place."

But it wasn't her use of Old Klingon obedience modes that made her recuperate so quickly over the next day or two, Kirk realized. When she first got out of bed, she was weak and shaky. What made her well was the medication the Klingon doctors had given her, her strong Klingon constitution, and Kirk's company. *I'm in love with a Klingon women,* he thought, and it was still a source of wonder, *and she's in love with me, and it's my very presence that enables her to overcome her illness.*

Even so, he thought that Bones McCoy would delight in the study of all these new Klingon biochemical discoveries. *What they can do with their own biochemistry!* he marveled. *What Leonard wouldn't give to know all about it!*

"Welcome aboard *Enterprise,* Mr. Tindall," Spock said, stepping off the transporter platform.

"Thank you, Mr. Spock," Elliott said, picking up his bags. To be aboard a Federation starship! This was more than he could have hoped for. He must make sure to take advantage of it to the fullest. He glanced around quickly, taking in and memorizing every detail.

"Mr. Tindall, your attention please," Spock said. A young woman stood crisply at attention by his side. "This is Lt. Crandall. She will show you your quarters, and then help you install the testing equipment in the engineering laboratories."

"A pleasure, Mr. Tindall," Ginny Crandall said, extending her hand. She was a slightly built young woman, in her late twenties, Elliot guessed, with close-cropped blond hair and piercing blue eyes.

"Lieutenant," Elliott nodded, taking her hand.

"If you will excuse me," Spock said. "Mr. Tindall, I will stop by to check on your progress shortly. In the meantime, I will be on the bridge." He turned and left the transporter room.

"Can I help you with one of those?" Ginny asked, indicating his bags.

"Thanks," Elliott said, handing her his duffel. "I really just need to make a quick stop at my quarters to change," and take my medicine, he added silently, "and then I'll want to get right to work."

Ginny smiled. "I can see why Mr. Spock went to such lengths to get you as his assistant," she said, leading him out of the transporter room and into a turbo elevator. "Deck 6," she said. "You sound as committed to your work as he is."

"Oh, I am," Elliot said. He smiled back at her. "What about your work, Lieutenant? What are your duties aboard this ship?"

"Weapons and Defense." The lift doors slid open. "Senior technician," she added, stepping out into the corridor.

Elliot started to follow, then groaned involuntarily as a stabbing pain lanced through his skull.

"Mr. Tindall?" Ginny turned back to face him. "Is something the matter?"

"No, I'm fine—just a long trip, I guess. Must've taken a little more out of me than I thought." He kept his voice steady, but his heart was pounding. He had taken twice his normal dosage just before he and Spock had boarded the shuttle from Earth: if his medicine was losing its potency this rapidly, he would be unable to function with any degree of effectiveness before long.

"If you like, we could stop at Sickbay and pick up something for the pain," Ginny offered.

"I said I was fine," Elliott insisted, a little more harshly than he intended. Ginny started involuntarily.

"Forgive me," he said. "Please. I get these . . . headaches occasionally, and I'm afraid I don't deal with them too well."

"I understand," she said, smiling. "Let me know if there's anything I can do."

He forced himself to return her smile. "You were telling me about your work, Lieutenant," he prompted.

"Please," she said. "Call me Ginny."

Chapter Twelve

KIRK AND KALRIND resumed their explorations—and found more out-of-bounds areas. Moreover, these areas were designated with signs reading

• RESTRICTED •
AUTHORIZED PERSONNEL ONLY
PAST THIS POINT

in both English and Klingonese. Intrigued, Kirk led the way back to the guarded area they had found first. The guards were gone now, and instead there was one of those bilingual signs, mounted since the last time the two had come this way.

"Now, that's interesting," Kirk said. "It's strange enough that you have restricted areas, given the peacefulness of your century. It's even stranger that the signs are written in English as well as your own language. Why is that?"

Kalrind shrugged. "I have no explanation. You'll have to ask Morith."

But when they managed to track him down in the ship's engineering section, Morith clearly resented being questioned about the matter. "You should be asking a military man, not a physicist," he rebuked them. "Oh, all right, then. The reason for using both languages is that we often have Federation people traveling on our ships, so signs are generally written in the official language of the Federation, as well as in Klingonese."

Kirk looked around at the humming machines and busy technicians. "And you don't want them going where they're not supposed to?" he asked.

Morith grimaced. "The universe has not changed in every detail in the last hundred years, Jim. Some things remain as they were in your day—including some of the things we all wish could change. We still have government secrets that the ordinary citizen is not allowed to know about, our citizens as well as yours."

"But there aren't any members of the Federation in this fleet. At least, I haven't seen or heard of any."

Morith nodded. "You're right, Jim. There aren't. Not that we didn't have requests from all over the Federation. Soldiers, scientists, diplomats, historians—they all wanted to join us. A plum assignment! But there's danger, as you know. If things don't work out, there could even be shooting between our ships and those of the Federation. The Federation in this time, I mean, your time. We simply couldn't risk their lives. Besides"—he drew himself up proudly—"this is *our* fight. This is, above all, the cause of the New Klingons against the Old."

As Kirk and Kalrind left the engineering section, Kirk mulled over what Morith had said. Earlier, Kalrind had explained why he had encountered no one but Klingons on the base where he had first found himself. The base was an out-of-the-way place, normally used for routine work, not prestigious enough to attract researchers from the Federation, Kalrind had said. She had further explained that he had been taken there to recover because of the budding plan to send this fleet back in time, with him on it, and the base had been so convenient a place from which to launch the fleet.

Well and good, and he could accept all of that, but if he was the *only* being on the fleet whose native language was not Klingonese, then the English on a newly emplaced bilingual warning sign was really aimed at him, wasn't it? A simple verbal warning would have been simpler and easier than putting up that sign.

I'm probably overreacting. The explanation is no doubt something simple enough. He could even think of one such explanation himself: that general-purpose, bilingual warning signs were readily available, and so one of those had been used.

No, Kirk assured himself, *there really is something just a bit facile about Morith's explanations. There's something he's not telling me.* That wasn't logic; it was intuition. Spock would have frowned at his thinking. McCoy would have applauded it. They were both wrong, of course. A commander could not function only at the intellectual level, could not ignore the processing of data constantly being performed by the mysterious deeper levels of his mind, any more than he could ignore logic and let himself be ruled by emotion. Kirk had always relied on both, always blended them, as in a parallel fashion he had relied for advice on both Spock and McCoy. He was still a commander—and he would therefore continue to be guided by that old, highly reliable mixture of reason and intuition.

Besides all that, more than Kirk's curiosity was

being piqued by those signs. If they truly *were* aimed only at him, then Morith must think that Kirk was the sort who placidly followed orders, whether or not he agreed with them, that he would suppress his curiosity because a sign told him to. Morith should have known better. *I'll have to find out just what it is he doesn't want me to see.*

Kalrind was deeply asleep, breathing shallowly and evenly. Kirk watched her for a while and listened to her, and then, satisfied, slipped out of bed, into his clothes, and out the door.

Once in the hallway, he walked rapidly, making no effort to be quiet. He had decided that his best chance to reach his destination without being stopped was not to act furtive but rather to march with head up, shoulders back, and face untroubled. *Easier said than done,* he thought.

Ship's time decreed it to be night, and Kirk met few Klingons on his way. Those he did pass seemed preoccupied and paid him little attention—he had hoped.

Eventually he reached the area he had targeted for inspection. Kirk had chosen it because of the plethora of warning signs, reasoning that the importance of whatever was hidden in such a section of the ship must be in direct proportion to the number of signs warning people away from it. It was also the corridor where he had encountered the Organian only a few days earlier, a coincidence that only made the place seem more important.

Kirk passed by the last of the signs and found himself facing a door guarded by an enormous Klingon wearing a uniform.

It was a uniform quite familiar to him. This aspect of Klingon society had not changed in a hundred years. Morith and the other New Klingons didn't wear uniforms, and so the presence of one was all the more startling.

Nor was that the only Old Klingon aspect to this guard. As soon as he saw Kirk, he glowered at him and said with a heavy Klingonese accent, "Human! Go away!" The Klingon stepped forward threateningly, drawing his disruptor from his belt.

Kirk smiled placatingly, holding up his hands to demonstrate peaceful intent and absence of weapon. As the guard hesitated, concentrating on Kirk's hands, Kirk kicked him hard in the groin.

The Klingon doubled over with a burbling cry, and Kirk knocked him to the floor with a two-handed downward chop on the back of his head. As the guard lay dazed on the floor, moaning, Kirk picked up the disruptor, which had fallen from the man's hand, set it to stun, and shot the guard with it.

Now I'll have some time to look around.

He dragged the unconscious Klingon through the doorway he had been guarding and dumped him in the center of the room beyond. He straightened up and looked around, instantly recognizing what the room was. Beyond a doubt, Kirk thought, this was a fire control center.

On Klingon ships, as on Starfleet ships, the firing of weapons was normally controlled from the bridge. Klingon ships, however, traditionally had at least one auxiliary room from which the main ship's weapons could be controlled; this was intended for backup, in case the bridge became inoperative during an attack— or before a Klingon-initiated attack. The standard layout of Klingon ships of various types, including such details as fire control centers, was well known from careful study of captured enemy ships, and Kirk was thus as familiar with the details of their design and construction and operation as any other Starfleet commander—perhaps almost as familiar as a Klingon commander. He was quite sure about this room.

Of course, he reminded himself, Morith had told him that the fleet was made up of old ships, leftovers from the violent past. The old fire control centers would therefore also still be part of the ships. But if this room was here only because it was a leftover, then why bother guarding it? And why were all the consoles so clean and dust-free, and why were the displays all active; in other words, why was this room being maintained, being kept in a ready condition?

And there was more. There was a monitor set into the console in front of him. Kirk stepped over to the console and fiddled with the controls. He found the one that changed the view on the monitor, and after experimenting, he turned to a setting that gave him a view of a launch bay filled with strike craft. These were the Klingon landing vehicles, used for quick and deadly assaults on enemy ground targets. *What,* he asked himself, *are these doing here?* Since that was an unanswerable question, he decided to press on.

At the far end of the room was another door. *Now, that's unusual,* Kirk thought, intrigued. An inner room was not standard in the normal fire control center of a Klingon ship. Sparing time only for a brief examination of the fire control consoles, he passed on to the next room.

This was much smaller than the fire control room, and it held only one machine—a curious contraption, completely unknown to Kirk. The console was covered with buttons and dials, but everything was labeled in Klingonese. While Kirk could understand spoken Klingonese slightly, his reading knowledge of it was rudimentary. Nonetheless, he did recognize on one button the symbol *HoS*, for "power."

Kirk hesitated for only a moment and then pressed the button. He was rewarded by a hum of energy and a faint vibration in the machine. Lights of various colors appeared on the console, blinking for a while, then settling into a steady glow.

So what do I do next? Tentatively, he pressed another button.

Suddenly the room was bathed in brilliant light. Kirk looked up in amazement to see an Organian hovering in the air in the middle of the room, just beyond the machine Kirk had been fiddling with.

Kirk felt an instant of dread and shame, akin to that a small boy might feel when caught at mischief by an adult. At the same time, he was grateful for the machine, providing a barricade, inadequate though it would be if the Organian did indeed wish to punish him. But time passed and the Organian did and said nothing; it hung motionless before him.

At last Kirk decided that one of them had to open the conversation. He leaned forward and said, "You're—"

"You're—" the Organian interrupted, his voice calm, cool, unemotional, echoing from the walls.

"—probably wondering—"

"—probably wondering—" the Organian said, repeating Kirk's words a fraction of a second after him.

"—what I'm doing here," Kirk finished, with the Organian repeating his words almost as soon as he said them. "Well, well," Kirk said. The Organian said, "Well, well."

Kirk pressed the power button again on the console. The hum of energy disappeared and the glowing lights went out. And the Organian vanished.

"Kirk!"

For an instant, Kirk almost imagined the angry cry had come from the Organian after all, but it was Morith, standing in the doorway and shaking with rage. Looming behind him were two more enormous, uniformed Klingons. "You are not supposed to be here!" Morith shouted at Kirk.

"And the Organian was supposed to be real," Kirk replied, angry himself and not trying to hide it. "Not a fake, a simulation. Just what are you up to, Morith?"

With a great effort at self-control, Morith said more quietly, "We can't talk about it here." He gestured with his head at the two uniformed men. They glared at Kirk, then turned away and picked up the guard Kirk had earlier stunned. Carrying him, they went out into the hallway and left, taking time for one last surly, warning look at Kirk. *Good* esprit de corps, *anyway,* Kirk thought.

"Follow me," Morith said, and it seemed to Kirk that Morith's attitude was scarcely less hostile and dangerous than that of the two guards he had brought with him. Wordlessly, Morith led the way through the ship to his office next to the bridge.

The door slid shut behind them, and Morith seated himself behind his desk, gesturing Kirk toward one of the chairs in front of the desk. "I apologize for my anger, Jim," Morith said abruptly. "The area you were in is . . . sensitive. We keep it under constant surveillance. That's how we knew someone was in there—that and the sudden power drain."

Kirk nodded. "Must use a lot of power. Maintaining a fake Organian, I mean." He said no more and sat staring at Morith, waiting patiently for an explanation.

The Klingon had the grace to look embarrassed. "A subterfuge," he said at last. "And perhaps an unwise one." He looked away from Kirk and thought for a few seconds before continuing. "We are worried that, despite the evidence of history, your people may not receive us peacefully. We also know from history that the humans and the Klingons of your day were very quick to open fire on an enemy who crossed their frontier—especially so formidable a fleet as this one."

"I've told you that the Federation's ships don't shoot first. They ask questions first."

Morith nodded. "Yes, you've told us that. But how can we take the chance? What if they *do* shoot first, this time? We'll have to defend ourselves, won't we? Well, I'm trying to prevent such a situation, you see. I thought that the presence of an Organian on our ships, traveling with our fleet, combined with your voice, would prevent a tragic mishap."

"Galactic peace through lies and deception, in other words."

Morith spread his hands. "With so much at stake, how can we take chances?" He waited for Kirk to answer, but when Kirk said nothing, Morith continued. "I apologize again for my anger, Jim. You must understand how upset I was when I saw you on the monitor. Did I tell you that we have that area under surveillance at all times—and all other restricted areas, as well?"

"I believe you mentioned it, yes."

"Jim, we simply can't continue on this basis. I mean that we have to know that you will abide by our security regulations and not keep making attempts to get into restricted parts of the ship. I *must* have your promise on that."

Kirk gave his word.

"Fine!" Morith said heartily, standing up and holding out his hand. "Trust, after all, has been normal between humans and Klingons for the last hundred years."

Kirk shook Morith's hand, smiled, and strode out. But he was far from ready to give Morith his complete trust again.

"It doesn't make any sense, damn it," Kirk told Kalrind later. "None of it does. I'm certain Morith's up to something."

"Oh, Jim, come now—"

"Don't try to humor me," he snapped at her. "What about those uniformed guards? You've seen what they're like, too. Is that how New Klingons are supposed to behave?"

"No," she admitted. "They're a lot like recordings I've seen of Old Klingons. But there are some of them around in the Empire still, you know. It's only been a hundred years since my people got control. A lot of the others are still skulking around. Probably even dreaming of grabbing power again."

"Which implies that Morith is in contact with them and has brought a bunch of them onto this ship, in spite of what he said to me about Klanth and his crew."

Kalrind looked startled at this suggestion. "Why that—that would be terrible. Subversive!"

"Also, there's the 'Organian' and his planned use of it. Not very consistent with New Klingon idealism, is it?"

Kalrind shook her head and refused to meet Kirk's eyes.

"And it's also inconsistent with Morith's insistence that we adhere scrupulously to what's known from history about the Tholian Incident. He's been planning to use that Organian to change Federation minds, instead of relying on what history says actually happened."

"When you put it that way," Kalrind said reluctantly, "it does all seem very suspicious. So what are you going to do about it?"

Kirk grimaced. "I don't know. I don't know that there *is* anything I can do. But I'm certainly going to keep a close eye on that man, and I'm not going to believe whatever he tells me."

Kalrind touched his arm hesitantly. "At least you're not condemning all of us—all Klingons. Maybe Morith *is* up to something, as you said. If so, you know it's only him."

Kirk smiled at her. "Oh, I know that. I know I can trust you. There is that, anyway." *But Morith is the one in charge of this fleet.* He kept that thought to himself, not wanting to upset Kalrind more than he already had.

Chapter Thirteen

THE NORMAL FLOW of announcements and orders in Klingonese aboard *Alliance* was suddenly interrupted by one in English. "Captain Kirk, to the bridge!"

Kirk looked at the speaker in shock, suffering from a sudden sense of dislocation. Then he shook his head, laughed at himself, and headed for the bridge.

Morith was there already, sitting on the dais in the command chair, running his fleet. Kalrind was also there, standing beside Morith and leaning over to confer with him. They both looked up when Kirk entered. "Ah, Jim," Morith said. "Look." He pointed at the forward screen.

The starfield was motionless, indicating that *Alliance* was not moving. Scattered across the field were blinking lights, and as Kirk watched, more such lights appeared. He looked at Morith for an explanation. The Klingon wore a worried frown, which he managed to smooth out when he noticed Kirk looking at him. "Federation ships," he said. "Each blinking light is a Starfleet warship. Exactly as predicted by the past, Starfleet has sent ships to stop us. But I must admit I . . . didn't realize from what I'd read that it would be so large and powerful."

Kirk watched the Federation fleet building still further and was overcome by delight and a fierce desire to be on his own bridge once again. "Where are we?" he asked, keeping his voice as casual as he could. He was trembling with excitement and having trouble keeping it from showing.

"Near Tholia, just as history records. They approached with shields up, Jim!" He spoke angrily.

"Of course they did, Morith. A huge Klingon fleet, great numbers of warships, has just entered Federation space. The fleet assembled to meet the enemy would of course approach with shields raised."

Morith grumbled, "This is not a good start to the Great Peace! Naturally, we have ours up as well, just in case your friends start firing at us."

"They won't fire first," Kirk said angrily.

Morith turned to him. "This is obviously a violent age. I can't afford to take any chances. I'm responsible for this fleet, all of this equipment. All of these people, too. It's a heavy responsibility. You understand all of that, Jim, surely?"

Kirk forced a smile. "Of course."

One of the crewmen at a console below the dais said something.

"Ah!" Morith said. "An attempt at communication!" He issued an order in sharp, guttural Klingonese, and the image on the large forward screen rippled and changed and gave way to an image of Fleet Admiral De La Jolla sitting in a standard Starfleet ship's command chair.

De La Jolla jumped to his feet. "Jim Kirk! So those bastards *did* kidnap you!" He was an overweight, aging man, and his jowls shook with rage.

Kirk held up his hands. "No, no, Fed. Calm down. The situation's not what you're thinking." *They should have put someone calmer in command of that fleet.*

"We'll get you off there!" De La Jolla raged on. "If we have to—!" He stopped and fell back into his chair, his face purple. He had stopped talking only because his anger made him unable to say more.

Kirk tried to think of something to defuse his volatile colleague, but before he could come up with something, De La Jolla recovered enough to issue a low command to someone off screen. He then turned back to Kirk and shook his finger at him. "Now you just listen to this, young man. I've got someone here who will talk sense into you."

"Young man," Kirk thought. *I suppose that's why I like old Federico: he can be insufferable at times, and I've never been sure he's all that competent, but he's always called me "young man."*

The screen rippled and changed again, and this time when the image re-formed it showed Spock sitting in the command chair of the USS *Enterprise,* with Leonard McCoy standing beside him, hands behind his back.

"Spock! Bones!" Kirk had stepped forward as if about to try to jump through the screen to his ship.

McCoy stared at him with open mouth and said nothing. Spock raised one eyebrow and said, "Captain. I'm pleased to see you looking so well, even though I must admit to some surprise—"

"Spock, for God's sake!" McCoy burst out. "Jim! This is amazing! How did you—?"

"Later," Kirk said, laughing with delight. "You don't know how happy I am to see both of you. I've got a lot to tell you."

"We all have a lot to say to each other." It was Morith, looking at the two humans with analytical interest. "May I suggest a conference in an hour, after we've all had a chance to discuss matters among ourselves?"

"If you wish," Spock said. "However, I do have many questions to ask Captain Kirk. This is quite apart from any discussion you and my fleet commander may have with each other."

"All of that can come later," Morith said firmly. "We will stay just where we are, taking no action, and in one hour we will contact you again for further discussions. At that time, Captain Kirk will have a great deal to say to you." He said something in Klingonese, and the forward screen returned to its starfield display.

Kirk turned on Morith with uncontained anger. "Why did you interfere? Do you know how long it's been since I've seen my friends? How long I was convinced that I'd never see them again? Why didn't you let us talk to each other?"

"Please come to my office, Jim." Morith rose from his seat and issued an order. Another Klingon stepped up on the dais and took Morith's place in the command chair. He and Morith exchanged a few words in low tones, and then Morith led the way from the bridge.

His small office was crowded. Kalrind was there, as were quite a few people Kirk didn't recognize. It was Morith, though, who did the talking; the rest listened.

"Jim," he said in a soothing voice, a calm and even voice—the voice of a man guided by reason—"Jim, I understand how upset you must be. But I did have a good reason for not letting you speak with your friends. Please try to stay calm until I've finished explaining to you."

Kirk bit back the angry remark he had been preparing and gestured for Morith to continue.

"Thank you, Jim. You see, what has been bedeviling me is the possibility that we may somehow alter history, distort it. On the one hand, one can say that whatever we do or say right now, during this confrontation with the Starfleet ships, will automatically follow the historical record, simply because that is the record of what *did* happen. On the other hand, there are so many details not even recorded at all, since historical records are always selective and not all inclusive, and if we do something different, in one of those small details, might we not be creating a new, parallel universe, one in which the future is not the future we know, what we New Klingons think of as the present?"

"That's an old discussion," Kirk said, still angry, "an old dilemma. No one has yet come up with the answer."

"True enough. But at the moment, the question is of more than theoretical interest, isn't it?"

Kirk was beginning to find the Klingon's calmness and his calculatedly soothing voice maddening. "Well, then? What's your solution?"

Morith shook his head. "I don't really have one. I do, however, have a strong determination that I won't allow anything to happen that could alter the past. This incident that we're now involved in simply *must* work, *must* resolve itself properly! We are working on creating our present in the proper form, Jim. I was afraid you might say the wrong thing if I let you talk on, and that's why I interrupted you."

"But, damn it, how *can* I say the wrong thing?" Kirk exploded. "If I say it, it's automatically right. If not, we don't know, anyway. Anything else is a circular argument. Or are you planning to provide me with a script?"

He had meant that sarcastically, but Morith replied, "We did consider that. After all, your *exact* words aren't part of the historical record, but the general sense of what you said is. Even some of the phrases have been preserved. However, I decided that you might sound artificial to your comrades. Anyway, they'll find it hard enough to believe that a Klingon fleet has come on a peaceful mission; there's no reason to make it even harder for them to believe you by making them suspect that you've been drugged or coerced into saying what you will say."

"There you are, then. Problem's solved. Let's go back to the bridge and reestablish communications."

"But I also feel," Morith plowed on, "that you ought to know the outline of what you did say, so that you won't step beyond the boundaries. In particular, you said only that we had come to establish peace and that we are a new breed of Klingons now struggling for control of the Empire. You didn't tell them anything about time travel until you reached Earth. And I can see why, now. The time travel aspect would have destroyed any chance of the Starfleet commanders on the scene believing you."

Kirk hesitated and then said reluctantly, "You have a point. So maybe you were right to break communications when you did. All right, then. Anything else?"

Morith shook his head. "For the rest, we'll just have to rely on your saying the right thing because history says you did."

Kirk snorted. "Let's not get into that again, please." He hesitated a moment before adding, "History must have told you that my ship would be with the fleet. Why didn't you forewarn me?"

Morith spread his hands in a gesture of helplessness. "The same problem again, Jim. We wanted you to react naturally, spontaneously. We want you to react that way to everything that happens."

Kirk chose to let the matter drop, and the group filed out of Morith's office and back toward the bridge. *What else does he know that he's not telling me?* Kirk wondered. Various things had already undermined his trust in Morith. This conversation had served only to undermine that trust still further.

The conundrum posed by time travel was a genuine one, though, Kirk knew. He had chosen to let Edith Keeler die because of it—because, had she lived, she would have destroyed his world.

He understood Morith's fear all too well.

A meeting was under way on the Starfleet ships at the same time.

It was being held onboard USS *Nonsuch*, the hastily designated flagship of the Federation fleet assembled to halt the Klingon incursion, Fleet Admiral De La Jolla commanding. Assembled on the flagship via transporter were various high-ranking Starfleet officers from the ships of the fleet, and among them were Spock and Scott of *Enterprise*. Both men were outranked by the majority of the others present, but De La Jolla had included them as a courtesy, knowing of their personal stake in any decisions made regarding Captain Kirk. In fact, it was Spock who had suggested that the meeting be held—and because of their personal involvement with Kirk, De La Jolla hoped they could provide useful additional information or impressions regarding the hyperspace contact with the captain.

That Admiral De La Jolla could entertain such a hope showed that, despite his long Starfleet career, he had managed to avoid dealing with both Vulcans and temperamental Scotsmen.

"Well, Mr. Spock," De La Jolla asked. "Is he under duress, or not?"

"Inadequate information, Admiral," Spock said with a calm that immediately enraged the temperamental admiral. Scott, who had been scowling from the beginning of the meeting, exploded at De La Jolla's question. "Duress?" he shouted. "O' *course* the puir mon's under duress! He's held by th' cursed Klingons! We need t' talk aboot *rescue*, not *analysis!*"

De La Jolla stared at him, dumfounded. No one had yelled at him in years—not since he had become superior in rank to everyone he normally dealt with, in fact. Finally he found his voice and said, "Mr. Scott! You forget yourself!"

Scott drew in a deep breath in preparation for another outburst, and Spock, showing rare insight into human interactions, stepped in quickly to prevent his comrade from destroying his career. "Mr. Scott is understandably overwrought, Admiral, at the threat both to the Federation and to Captain Kirk. When he disappeared while aboard a Klingon vessel, we all naturally assumed that he had been kidnapped by the Klingons. That fear seems to have been justified."

"*Seems* t' hae been?" It was Scott, exploding again.

"Seems to have been," Spock repeated firmly. "That voice over hyperspace radio may have been a computer artifact, a simulacrum. We need to know more before we draw any conclusions or plan any actions."

De La Jolla said sarcastically, "That's all very well, Mr. Spock, but we have to do *some*thing!"

"Aye," Scott added, clearly surprised at being able to agree with De La Jolla.

"May I remind you that we *have* done something," Spock said. "We changed codes and dispositions throughout Starfleet precisely in case the captain was in enemy hands. And now we have something else to do: an hour has passed; it's time to resume contact with the Klingon fleet. I have some suggestions as to how you should proceed, Admiral, while speaking to the Klingon commander."

De La Jolla paused, and struggled to regain control of his temper. "Since you think you know what we should do, Spock—and because you know Captain Kirk better than any of us—I'm designating you the spokesman for the fleet. I'll be watching you, Spock. I want to see what *you* come up with."

On their way to the *Nonsuch* transporter room, Scott murmured, "How did a man with so little self-control rise so high?"

Spock glanced at him in momentary surprise before his face smoothed out again into its normal expressionlessness. "Theories abound, Mr. Scott, but I have inadequate data and refuse to speculate."

Scott snorted. "Well, tell me this, then. Why did you suggest that meeting? Nothing was accomplished."

"On the contrary, Mr. Scott, something very important was accomplished. I had hoped only to be a calming influence. To be appointed spokesman was more than I had thought possible. If Admiral De La Jolla were to speak for the fleet, I would have little hope of the captain escaping with his life. This way, I have at least a chance of bringing him back."

"Ah! So there *is* slyness and calculation behind that calm surface, eh?"

Spock pondered that as they walked in silence, approaching the door to the transporter room. They entered, still in silence, and climbed onto the transporter platform. Just as the first tinglings of the field were building up, Spock said, "Thank you for the compliment, Mr. Scott."

As soon as they had materialized on the transporter platform on *Enterprise,* Spock headed for the bridge and Scott for the Engineering Section.

Spock strode down the hallway and into a turbo elevator.

"Bridge."

His unemotional voice, as always, was a perfect mask, beneath which lay fear for his friend and commander, a perfectly logical fear that left no room for baseless optimism.

Elliot Tindall had no room for baseless optimism either. He was fighting a sea of hormones. His medication was wearing off; he needed no medical scan to tell him that. He had been under pressure from the moment he stepped aboard *Enterprise*. With each day, his mood worsened, and he swallowed his pills with a growing feeling of desperation.

For it was clear that the pills had ceased to have any effect.

Leonard McCoy was working grimly, even sullenly, on a pile of paperwork, trying to grind through it and get it off his desk, when Elliot burst in on him.

"Dr. McCoy?" he said harshly.

McCoy looked up from the form displayed on his

monitor. "I told Commander Chapel I was not to be disturbed," the doctor said politely.

"My name is Elliot Tindall," the newcomer hurriedly replied. "We haven't met—"

"I've heard of you," McCoy drawled. He stood up slowly and extended his hand. Had Elliot known it, this affectation of lazy, stereotypically Southern mannerisms on McCoy's part was a danger sign, a hint at the anger the doctor was hiding.

"Oh, yes." Elliott shook the proffered hand briefly. "I wonder if you could let me have some sort of sedative."

McCoy looked at him sharply. "A sedative?" Surprise and professional interest combined to chase away his anger at being interrupted. "Just what sort of problems are you having, young man?"

Elliot hesitated. Beneath his seemingly calm surface lay an overwhelming anger: for a moment, Elliot wanted to kill this man before him, this man with his penetrating looks, and simply take what he wanted. But the reasons for not doing so were sufficiently obvious to him—not the least being his ignorance about where drugs were kept down here—that he mastered his almost out-of-control emotions, and said, "Jumpiness. Short temper. With that fleet out there, this being my first deep-space assignment—I just need something to calm me down, to keep myself under better control."

McCoy snorted and seemed to lose interest. "You and everyone else. It's the long hours and the lack of sleep that do it. And the lack of exercise and the irregular, snatched meals. I'll call up Spock and order that Vulcan taskmaster to give you more time off and put you on a more regular schedule. That should do the trick—and much more safely than some chemicals. The body's ability to heal itself . . ."

Elliot smiled and nodded, sweated and clenched his fists, hidden from view by McCoy's desk. He would get nothing from this old idiot.

"Yes, I see, Doctor," he said when McCoy at last ran out of steam. "I'm sure you're right. I'll follow your suggestions. Thank you for your advice. Please don't disturb Mr. Spock, though. He's very busy and under considerable pressure himself. I'll speak to him when the time seems right."

"Hmph," McCoy said. "The time's never right for that overgrown leprechaun to take normal human frailties into account. But I'll honor your wishes, nonetheless, Mr. Tindall. Now get out of here and let me get back to work."

Normal human frailties! Elliott thought bitterly, hopelessly as he left the office. *Oh, Doctor, you can't imagine how deep they go!*

And now, how was he to manage? How could he hold on?

After Elliot had left, McCoy struggled with his conscience, lost, and called Spock on the bridge.

"Spock here."

The calm voice, as always, both grated on McCoy and made him feel indefinably inferior. He almost changed his mind and broke the connection, but then he thought better of it. "Listen, Spock, I'm of two minds about this. My respect for a patient's confidentiality is at war with my duty to his health."

"Hello, Doctor."

"Oh, yeah. Hello. Don't change the subject." He told Spock briefly about Elliot's visit and request. "He asked me not to bother you, but I've decided to, anyway. Stop driving the man so hard, Spock. He's not a Vulcan, you know. He's only human."

"No, Doctor, he's certainly not a Vulcan," Spock agreed. "How would you characterize his mental state?"

"Based on my extensive observation of him, you mean?" McCoy asked with heavy sarcasm.

"Yes, based on that."

"On the edge," McCoy said reluctantly. "Just barely holding it in check."

"Holding what in check, Doctor?"

"I don't know, Spock! My extensive observations only lasted for a few minutes, during which I did most of the talking. He's falling apart, though. I could tell that."

"Was that not sufficient grounds for you to order him relieved from duty, Doctor? Grounds enough, at least, for you to contact me?"

"Well, I *am* contacting you, damn it! Anyway, I can't be bothered with that until after this crisis is over. It's not as if the man is dangerous, you know. He's very English. If he goes over the edge, the worst outward sign will probably be that his grammar will deteriorate."

"Thank you for that very professional advice, Doctor," Spock said, frowning. He broke the connection.

"Mr. Spock?"

He swiveled his chair around to find himself facing a worried-looking Ginny Crandall, who had turned away from her console, seeking his attention.

"Yes, Lieutenant?"

"Is there something the matter with Ell—Mr. Tindall?" Ginny asked.

"It is, quite possibly, nothing, Lieutenant," Spock said.

"I hope so," Ginny said.

"As do I," Spock said, meeting her eyes. He swiveled back to face the forward viewscreen. "Please maintain a close watch on your monitor, Lieutenant. We are in the midst of a very delicate situation."

Chapter Fourteen

"GREETINGS TO the entire United Federation of Planets, and in particular to the commanders and crews of the valiant Starfleet ships sent to meet us. I am *Joh* Morith, commander of this fleet."

Listening to Morith's opening message, Kirk tried to imagine De La Jolla's reaction. He hoped the admiral wouldn't lose his temper to such a degree that he ordered his fleet to open fire on the Klingons. He had heard some astonishing stories in the past about the older man's actions while he was still commanding a starship.

But to his surprise and relief, it was Spock's face, and not that of the fleet admiral, that filled the screen at the front of *Alliance*'s bridge.

Morith finally finished and gestured for Kirk to come forward and speak.

"Hello, Spock," Kirk said.

A slight bow from the neck. "Captain."

"Spock, what I'm about to tell you will be hard to believe, but it's vital that you take my word. I've seen it at first hand. These people I'm with are not the Klingons you know. They call themselves the New Klingons . . ."

Throughout Kirk's narrative, Spock's face gave nothing away. When Kirk had finished, Spock said, "One moment, please, Captain." The screen went blank.

"Kirk!" Morith said. "What's going on? Are they going to attack us?"

"No! Just stay calm, Morith." He felt less sure of himself than he tried to appear. What *was* Spock up to?

The image on the screen re-formed. This time, the field of view was larger, and Leonard McCoy could be seen standing next to Spock's command chair and looking angry. Spock said, "As I'm sure you'll understand, Captain, before we can consider your remarkable story, we must be assured that you are truly speaking your own mind. Voice analysis indicates that you are not being coerced to say what you have just said; however, such analysis cannot prove that you have not been drugged. Dr. McCoy insists that he must have medical data on your current physical condition before he can make a decision in that regard. The simplest solution would be for us to beam you back onboard *Enterprise*."

Kirk's heart leapt at the thought: to be back on his ship, in his command chair. Then he looked at Morith, and the Klingon was scowling and shaking his head.

"Mr. Spock, what assurances do we have that your fleet will not then fire upon us? We cannot begin our peaceful relations on a basis of mistrust," Morith said. "*Believe* what Captain Kirk is telling you."

"Sir," Spock replied, "it is more important to find out if Captain Kirk truly believes what he is saying to us. Without that, we cannot proceed."

"Then here!" Morith snapped out an order in Klingonese. "I have ordered all our shields lowered. What more can I do to prove our intentions are peaceful?"

Kirk saw surprise on the faces of all his bridge crew. All save Spock, who merley raised an eyebrow.

"Most impressive—we will certainly take this into account in our discussions," the Vulcan said. He leaned sideways to listen to McCoy for a moment, then straightened and said to the screen, "Dr. McCoy wishes me to say, however, that he still insists on running a medical scan on the Captain."

"That wasn't all I said, Spock!" McCoy cut in.

Spock raised his hand to silence the doctor. "We are prepared to beam the Captain aboard at any time."

Morith said, "I'll be in contact shortly." He hit a button on the arm of his command chair and the screen went blank. "What do they want, Kirk? I've laid myself open to attack, and even that doesn't satisfy them!"

"They told you what they want," Kirk reminded him. "I think they want to believe me, but they need something definite to allay their suspicions. And don't forget that they must give very good reasons for their actions to Starfleet Command—especially if those actions include inviting a Klingon fleet to Earth." Kirk smiled. "You have to give them something they can use with both Starfleet Command and the Federation Council."

"I see, I see . . ." Morith stared thoughtfully at the blank screen. "Yes, Jim, you're right: those are ramifications I hadn't been aware of. The Empire is very different—even now." He pondered the problem for a while, then said, "Frankly, though, I still don't know how far I can trust them. I still want you onboard to discourage an attack. I have a compromise suggestion for them."

He thumbed a button his chair arm and the screen lit up again, showing Spock and McCoy still in discussion on the bridge of the *Enterprise*. Spock looked up in polite interest at a signal from Uhura. "Yes, Lord Morith?"

Morith spoke without any of the formalities or excessive politeness he had adopted at the beginning. "I am prepared to transmit a complete medical scan of Captain Kirk to your ship's computer. Our doctors are surely as competent at performing such a scan as yours are. I can offer no more."

This time it was Spock who said he would be in touch again soon, and contact was broken from his end. As the *Enterprise* bridge faded away, Kirk could see McCoy gesticulating angrily and speaking rapidly. However, he could hear nothing.

Long, tense minutes followed on the Klingon ship. No one spoke. Finally Spock made contact again. McCoy was no longer in view. "Dr. McCoy will agree to your suggestion only if he can perform the scan personally. He has gone to the transporter room and has ordered his portable scanner sent there. He is prepared to beam over as soon as you give your permission."

Morith looked at Kirk with an exasperated expression. Kirk shrugged and raised both hands, palms up. "All right, then," Morith said. "Whenever you're ready, you may transport your doctor over. But tell him to leave his equipment behind. We'll provide the medical scanner. We want him to use equipment we know we can trust."

McCoy stepped off the transporter platform and looked around with a skeptical air. "So *this* is what a new Klingon warship looks like from the inside. I'm not impressed."

Kirk shook his head, smiling. "What would it take to impress you, Bones?"

"You showing up healthy and normal on my own scanning equipment," McCoy said bluntly. "How are you, Jim?"

"All things considered, remarkably well, Doctor."

"All things?" McCoy came up close to Kirk, staring intently into his face. "Been wearing your glasses?"

Kirk gestured impatiently. "No, damn you. Of course not. They're still back on *Enterprise*. And before you ask, yes, it has been giving me headaches."

McCoy grinned. "Good. Now I know it's you and not some sort of Klingon impersonator."

Kirk shook his head in exasperation but couldn't help grinning. "Bones, you can't imagine how good it is to see you."

"Oh, yes, I can, Jim," McCoy said soberly.

Kirk turned away, hiding the rush of emotion McCoy's words had engendered. "We'll have to use the ship's Sickbay. It's a lot smaller than the one you're used to on *Enterprise*. Come on. I'll lead the way."

McCoy passed the scanner over Kirk, grumbling to himself. "Awful equipment. Primitive. How do they take care of their own? At least it's labeled in English as well as Klingonese. Electrolytes're low. That's funny." He tapped the scanner a couple of times with his forefinger. "Unreliable junk. Says here you're reverting to adolescence, Jim boy. What've you been up to?"

"You wouldn't believe me if I told you, Bones," Kirk said uncomfortably.

"Try me."

"Maybe when all of this is over. Well? Are you satisfied that I'm really James Kirk and in my right mind?"

"Oh, you're James Kirk, all right," McCoy

drawled. "As for being in your right mind, I've never been too sure of that. But you're your own man right now, I'd testify to that."

"Wonderful?" Kirk hopped down from the examining table and began pulling on his shirt again without waiting for McCoy's permission. "That's exactly what I want you to do."

"Whoa, there. Hold on a minute. I just happen to have brought something of my own with me, in spite of what your heavy-browed friend said." McCoy reached under his uniform shirt and brought out a hypospray.

"Now what?"

"It's those pesky electrolytes. Been having some trouble with your thinking processes?" He looked intently at Jim. "Loss of concentration, maybe even some dizzy spells?"

"Now that you mention it, how did you know that—?"

"Shut up and hold still." So saying, McCoy applied the hypospray to Kirk's upper arm. "That should help."

"It does already," Kirk admitted. "Hurt, though. You're losing your touch, Bones."

"Hmph." McCoy rubbed the spot where he had applied the hypospray. "Feel anything?"

"Smarts like the devil!"

"Uh-huh." McCoy nodded. "As the old country doctor I was apprenticed to used to say—"

Kirk interrupted triumphantly. "Who never existed. You went to a medical school, like everyone else. Really, Bones, how long has it been since there were any old country doctors on Earth, or since anyone apprenticed for his medical training?"

"Too long," McCoy snapped back. "Okay, okay.

You're fine. Healthy as the proverbial horse—although that's a strange proverb, considering some of the horses I've known."

"Careful, Bones. I'm still your commanding officer."

"Nope. You're a POW. So, what now?"

"Now you go back to *Enterprise* and tell everyone that I'm in my right mind and should be believed."

McCoy nodded slowly. "Is that you want me to do?"

Kirk nodded.

"Okay. Now, about my fee . . . "

Kirk gripped McCoy's elbow and began steering him toward the door. "As Shakespeare said, 'He is well paid that is well satisfied.' "

"You're assuming I'm well satisfied."

Kalrind chose that moment to enter Sickbay. She looked at McCoy anxiously. "You're the human doctor. Is Jim all right?"

McCoy looked back and forth between the two of them, his eyes narrowed analytically. "Hmm. And you are?"

"Kalrind, Doctor. A friend of Jim's," she added quickly.

"Y-e-e-s," McCoy said slowly. "He has a talent for making friends. I think he's all right. I have to take the data back with me and analyze it before I can say for sure." He turned to Kirk. "How about this one, Jim: 'A man at sixteen may be a boy at sixty.' "

Kirk groaned in theatrical despair and steered McCoy toward the door again. "I'll be back as soon as I get rid of this burr under my saddle," he called to Kalrind, who looked puzzled, and exited with McCoy still firmly under control.

When they reached the transporter room, Kirk said, "Prejudices left over from your ancestors, Bones?"

But McCoy refused to be provoked. "Just don't worry about the mote in my eye, Jim. If you need help, just use my name."

He stepped onto the platform, carrying the wafer recordings of his scan of Kirk, and signaled to the technician running the transporter.

"Mote in my eye, Jim boy," he repeated, and disppeared in a column of twinkling light.

Kirk shrugged his shoulders in puzzlement and left the transporter room.

"Well, Doctor?"

McCoy turned at the familiar voice, calm and deliberate as always. For all his goading of the Vulcan over the years, McCoy still has no idea whether Spock really felt no emotion or simply did a superb job of disguising any he did feel. "Here it is." He gestured at the pile of computer printout on the desk before him.

"Paper, Doctor?"

"Now, don't start, Spock! You know I like something I can pick up and hold. And fold and rub between my fingers and scribble on."

"As you have on this, I see. What do you wish me to do with this stack of paper?"

"Look at it. Read it. Examine it. Draw conclusions from it."

One Vulcan eyebrow rose. "I was under the impression that such analysis was one of your duties, Doctor. The commander of a starship does have other duties."

"Right now, Spock," McCoy said angrily, "your main duty seems to be to stare at the Klingon fleet commander and hope that he blinks first. Well, then, I'll tell you what you'll find if you examine these papers: nothing."

"Thank you, Doctor." Spock turned to go.

"Wait! All right, all right. I was being deliberately obscure, I admit it. Are you happy now?"

"Doctor, is there a point to all of this? Despite the impression you may have received, I *do* have duties other than trying to stare the Klingon commander down."

"Oh, Spock, hold on! I'm trying to be open with you. What I was getting at is that on the face of it, the scanner recordings look okay. They seem to indicate that Jim is just fine, perfectly healthy, what and who he seems to be, speaking and acting his own mind."

"By 'seem to indicate,' I assume you mean that they don't really indicate that?"

"Not that I can prove objectively," McCoy said grudgingly. "I've analyzed the data pretty thoroughly. It wasn't exactly that I saw anomalies in it. In fact, everything was perfectly consistent. I'd say it was *too* perfect, except I know how you'd react to that sort of statement. Anyway, I didn't like it. It rang alarm bells in my intuition. The more I looked at it, the deeper I went into it, the more I felt that way. That's when I got alarmed and called you."

To Spock, of course, instrument data were virtually sacred. If the instruments were working properly and properly calibrated, then their results should logically be accepted before the inexact and questionable measurements taken by human senses—and certainly before the suspicions of a human who had always been suspicious of all instruments. "Doctor," he said carefully, "can you point out to me actually conflicting readings? Your intuition is not reason enough for me to take action."

McCoy jumped to his feet, trembling with anger. "You listen to me, Spock. I *know* Jim Kirk! I've known him both as a friend and as his doctor for many years, and my intuitions about these readings are reliable. Something bad is happening to that man. You're his friend, too. That means you have a special responsibility to him, in addition to your duty as commander of this ship. You've got to listen to me and forget about logic. You've got to *do* something. Jim's life may be in danger over there."

"I hardly think so, Doctor. The Klingons have had ample time already to injure the captain, if that is what they wish to do." But inwardly, Spock was reconsidering what McCoy had said. He had learned long ago, from ample observation of James Kirk, not to dismiss human intuition as valueless. Moreover, despite their constant sniping at each other, he had a high opinion of McCoy's competence.

And there was more. In the light of what Spock had spent his time in San Francisco proving, McCoy's suspicions carried considerable weight with him.

There was also the matter of his own impressions during his conversations with Kirk and Morith. He disliked having to trust intuition, but in this case he had no other data to depend on. He had not been satisfied with those conversations. He felt that communication with Kirk had not been completely free and open. He also felt that he could not trust Morith.

Even without what he had discovered during his investigations on Starbase Seventeen and Earth, he would have felt these misgivings.

McCoy fidgeted nervously. "Spock, I can practically hear the relays clicking in that computer you call a brain," he said.

"Relays, Doctor?" Spock replied. "You've been reading historical novels again." He stood. "I must follow logic, doctor—or reason, if you prefer. Logic, reason, common sense: all dictate that I should accept Captain Kirk's apparent health and clarity of mind as being precisely that. I shall proceed on that basis. All that is required is that you enter your certification of the captain's mental health in the records."

McCoy grinned and shook his head slowly without saying a word.

Spock stared at him for a moment, then said, "I shall humor you, Dr. McCoy. What do you require in order to give me that certification?"

"Just what I asked for in the first place; no more than that. I want to examine Jim here, with my own equipment, in my own Sickbay. No Klingon machines, and no Klingons hanging around."

"I doubt if Morith would agree to that."

"Then you don't agree to letting his ships pass. Not without a fight, anyway."

Spock considered, not for the first time, how ready humans were to engage in bloodshed in contradiction to their frequent professions of a love of peace. Nonetheless, no matter how offended he might be by McCoy's attitude, he had little choice but to bow before the man's demands. "I shall relay your request to Morith, but I consider it unlikely that he will accede."

McCoy smiled again.

"Was there anything else, Doctor?" Spock asked.

"No—yes, wait a minute." McCoy snapped his fingers. "Tindall. He called again and asked for a sedative. Spock, I thought you were going to take it easier on that young man."

"Indeed." Spock was silent for a moment. Finally he spoke. "If my suspicions are correct, no amount of sedatives will help Mr. Tindall." He turned and left Sickbay.

McCoy watched him go.

"Now what in hell is that supposed to mean?"

Elliot tossed and turned fitfully on his bunk. The doctor's drugs wouldn't have done him any good anyway, he realized. The real problem was that his own medication seemed to have lost its strength during the years, and the only way he could remedy that was to replace his pills with new versions of the same thing—stronger ones. Surely there had been advances since he had been given his supply; surely there were now more powerful and effective drugs available for those in his position.

That meant there was only one place he could go for help.

He drew a deep breath, held it, trying to force some sort of calm into his nerves, to still the waves of unreason and violence that had been coursing through him at random intervals for hours now. At last, he felt calm enough to head for his goal. He left his cabin, and headed for the nearest turbo elevator.

It shouldn't take him long to get where he was going, fortunately, since his destination was also in the starship's primary hull. He could make it that far, he was sure.

Then the turbo elevator opened, and he found himself face-to-face with Ginny Crandall.

"Elliot?" she said. "I thought I'd stop by and see how you were—"

He shrank from her, his nerves suddenly a-jangle. There was a shrill, piercing noise, like a high-speed drill. His vision blurred, till he could scarcely make out her face, let alone recognize it.

"What's wrong?" Ginny asked anxiously. "Should I call Medical?"

"That noise." Elliot groaned. "What is it?"

"Noise—oh, my communicator. It's been malfunctioning for days. I can't even hear it—too high-pitched. My roommate keeps complaining about it, but she's a Sezanian. You're the only human I know who can hear it."

As Elliot staggered, she instinctively reached for him. He pushed her hands away frantically. "Don't touch me!" he yelled. Ginny gasped and stepped back.

This was all wrong, Elliot thought. He was losing control again: he could see the concern in Ginny's eyes.

Ginny stepped toward him. "Elliot," she began hesitantly. "You need help. Listen . . ."

"No!" he howled, shoving Ginny aside. She slammed hard into the bulkhead, and sank to the floor.

Elliot ran as fast as he could down one corridor, then another, trying to escape the noise that grated in his ears. At last he stopped to catch his breath.

Slowly, he recovered his senses and resumed the journey toward his earlier goal.

Chapter Fifteen

KIRK WAS IN *Alliance*'s gymnasium with Kalrind, still working on rebuilding his strength. They were gripping each other's exercise suit, laughing as each tried to throw the other.

"Stop playing those stupid games!"

Kirk looked up to see Morith, visibly furious, standing in the doorway. "Kirk, your people are increasing their demands!"

Morith calmed down enough to tell them of Spock's latest demand that Kirk beam to *Enterprise* for another medical scan.

"What harm could it do?" Kirk said in what he hoped was a reasonable tone. "And it could do a lot of good. Obviously, since nothing has happened for so long, we're not making any real progress. One side has to make a move. Starfleet is actually considering escorting this enormous fleet to Earth, to the heart of the Federation, but you've got to offer something in return. All they're really asking for is assurance about me and what I've told them."

"And then they'll make another new demand!" Morith said. "When will it end, Kirk?" He raised his hands unconsciously, his fingers opened and tense. "When will it end?"

Kirk stepped back from him, suddenly on the alert for an attack, amazed at the same time that he could get such a feeling about Morith, of all people. "We're not like that, Morith. You're going to have to trust my judgment on that, just as you're asking us to trust you." Inspiration struck him. "You know, if I could go over and take Kalrind with me, that would really make an impression. Their first meeting with a genuine New Klingon! We could show them in a very concrete way just who and what the New Klingons really are. That might be enough to seal the decision right then and there."

"That's a wonderful idea!" Kalrind broke in. "I'd love to visit a human ship!"

Morith glared at her. "Out of the question. I can't expose you to that risk."

Kalrind drew herself up. Suddenly she was a martial figure and not an academic one. "You have no right to—"

"I am your commander!" Morith's voice cracked across the gymnasium. "To you, here and now, I am your Emperor!"

Kalrind shrank back and turned her face aside, not meeting Morith's eyes. Kirk watched the interplay with great interest. "You know that she wouldn't be in any danger on a Starfleet ship," he said.

Morith stared at him silently, eyes narrowed, face tight with anger. "No such trip by you is mentioned in the historical accounts of the Tholian Incident."

"Interesting—but irrelevant. The fact that the historical accounts do not mention that I beamed over to *Enterprise* is not at all the same as their stating that I did not beam over, is it? Do they say specifically that I did *not* beam over?"

Morith stared at him silently again, his face expressionless. Finally he said, "This discussion is at an end," and turned and stalked from the gymnasium.

Elliot burst into the transporter room, startling the technician at the controls. "Sir?" the man said uncertainly, looking Elliot's civilian clothes up and down. "Can I help you?"

"Beam me over," he snarled, feeling an unreasoning hostility toward the young technician.

"Over where, sir?"

"The Klingon flagship!" Elliot bellowed. "Right now!" He lurched toward the transporter platform.

"I'm afraid I can't do that without authorization from the bridge, sir." The technician said hesitantly. "You're Mr. Spock's new assistant, aren't you?"

Elliot nodded wordlessly.

"Would you like me to call the bridge and verify the authorization, sir?" the technician asked. He reached below the console and pressed a button.

Elliot stood still in the center of the room, directly in front of the transporter platform, staring at the technician and swaying from side to side. He hunched his shoulders and moved toward the technician, growling deep in his throat, a low-pitched, rumbling sound. "Fool!" he said. "Obey me!"

For a moment, the technician held his station behind the transporter controls as Elliot advanced on him. Finally, though, he broke and made for the door.

Elliot was there before him. He swung clumsily at the technician, his hand open, the fingers curved like claws, rather than closed into a fist. The technician dodged.

Elliot was moving slowly and clumsily, his eyes roaming the room. He tried to focus in on the technician—all he could feel was an overpowering need for his medication.

"Don't make me hurt you, sir," the technician said. "Let me call the bridge, or Dr. McCoy—"

Elliot lunged again, this time much quicker. The technician stepped expertly aside, and threw a quick punch, connecting solidly with Elliot's cheekbone. Elliot barely felt it, advancing with a snarl.

The young man dodged, stepping behind Elliot as he moved past, then threw his left arm around Elliot's neck, locking the hold tight by grasping his left wrist with his right hand. Elliot twisted and slipped out of the hold. Now he could see the beginnings of fear in the technician's eyes. His opponent jumped back frantically, but Elliot pursued him, closed his hands around the fellow's throat, and squeezed viciously.

The door to the transporter room swished open. Men in the uniform of the Security Department crowded into the room, phasers drawn.

"Let him go, Tindall!" one said.

Elliot looked uncomprehendingly at him, still gripping the neck of the transporter technician.

"I'll shoot!" the Security man shouted at him.

Elliot slowly loosened his grasp and let the unconscious transporter technician slide to the floor. "Aah," he said in a low, stretched-out whisper. He turned from the unmoving technician and advanced on the Security team.

"Stay there! Freeze, damn it!"

Elliot ignored their words and kept moving toward them. Without a warning, without the merest hint, he leaped forward.

Before they could shoot, he was among them, chopping with rigid hands to right and left. They couldn't shoot at him without hitting their comrades. They tried to dodge, to use hand-to-hand combat against him, but even when blows landed, Elliot was oblivious to them.

The door swished open again, and Spock stepped through. Two of the Security men were on the floor, unmoving, and the other two were clearly outmanned by their single, crazed opponent. "Mr. Tindall!" Spock said sharply.

Elliot turned to him, uncomprehending.

"Mr. Tindall!" Spock said again. "Control yourself!"

Elliot threw a punch directly at his face. Spock moved his head fractionally aside and the blow *whsshed* past harmlessly. He grabbed Elliot's wrist, bent the arm down and then up behind Elliot's back. During the instant when Elliot was immobilized with his back to him, Spock dropped his free hand lightly upon a point where Elliot's neck and shoulder met and squeezed.

Elliot dropped heavily to the floor, unconscious. Spock stepped back and away from him. He looked at the two Security men still on their feet. "Take this man to a holding cell. I'll call Sickbay."

After Spock had placed the call, he turned his attention to the transporter technician. The man was stirring and groaning on the floor, fingering his bruised throat cautiously.

Spock kneeled beside him. "Can you understand me?" Spock asked calmly.

"Yes, sir." The voice was a whisper.

"Talk as little as possible," Spock instructed him. "Help has been summoned. I must know: where did Mr. Tindall wish to be transported?"

The technician coughed a couple of times, cleared his throat, and at last managed to say, "Klingon flagship."

Spock regained his feet. Only one who knew him well, such as James Kirk, could have detected the sadness in his face.

At first McCoy objected loudly to Tindall's imprisonment. He felt Elliot should be under his care in Sickbay. He came to Spock's quarters, hoping to convince the Vulcan of that. So Spock, who had hoped to keep the matter quiet, had to explain his motivations to the doctor.

First he described the scene in the transporter room.

"Well," McCoy said grudgingly, "it does seem pretty suspicious. But there's obviously something wrong with the man, Spock."

"Indeed," Spock said, with a hint of sarcasm. "Let me show you what that something is, Doctor." He turned his chair toward the computer terminal. "Computer."

"Working."

"Display file DISASTER."

McCoy tried to raise one eyebrow in Vulcan manner to indicate that he thought Spock's choice of file name overly melodramatic, but then the display that had appeared caught his eye. He frowned as he leaned forward and read it over Spock's shoulder. "You've got Tindall's name on here. And others I don't recognize."

"Down the left-hand side of the screen," Spock agreed. "And in the column to the right?"

"I don't recognize—aah! They're place names." He straightened up again. "But I don't see what you're getting at, Spock."

"Surely those place names jog your memory, Doctor."

McCoy grumbled something even Spock's Vulcan

hearing couldn't pick up and read the screen again. "Devon, Archangel, New Athens, . . ." He turned toward Spock, looking startled. "Great disasters, all of them. The Devon Disaster, the nuclear power station at Archangel, the matter–antimatter explosion on Centaurus. Towns and cities wiped out, lives lost. That last one, especially, I'm not likely to forget. All right, Spock. Enough. Explain."

Spock nodded. "Gladly, Doctor. As you said, the places named on the right were all the sites of terrible disasters, some natural and some manmade, throughout the Federation. What they have in common is the great loss of life. The names on the left are those of people who have attained high positions in Starfleet or the Federation government. The place names show where those men and women were born."

McCoy said in bewilderment, "So what? I admit it's a very strange coincidence. Or maybe the destruction of their home towns gave those people a kind of drive that led them to their current high-level jobs. But beyond that—say," he said, interrupting himself, "just how did you get that information? I thought personal data was confidential?"

"I was able to obtain an extract from Starfleet and Federation personnel records while I was in San Francisco."

McCoy grinned at him. " 'Obtained,' eh? Do you maybe mean 'stole'? Easy enough for a computer expert like you, huh?"

"Can we return to the results I show on the screen, Doctor? The significance of what I have found may be enormous."

"How do you mean?" McCoy asked.

Spock told him.

As the Vulcan spoke, McCoy progressed from incredulity to fear. Finally he interrupted Spock's explanation by jumping to his feet and saying angrily, "Why're you sitting here calmly and telling *me* all of this? Contact Starfleet Command right away and let them know!"

"We need one more piece of evidence before we can offer a solid enough case, Doctor."

"And you expect Tindall to provide that missing piece?"

"Exactly," Spock nodded.

McCoy frowned. "Spock—did you know about Tindall all along, or . . ." He let the sentence trail off.

"Mr. Tindall's erratic behavior prompted my suspicions," Spock said, "but all this"—he nodded toward the computer screen—"was speculation until the incident in the transporter room."

"I see," McCoy said. "Well. I'll get right on it." He headed for the door.

"One moment, Doctor. You'll need a Security team."

"What? Rubbish, Spock!" McCoy waved him off.

Instead of answering, Spock issued a command to the computer, and the listing of names and places disappeared, to be replaced by a view of Tindall's holding cell.

"Good God!" McCoy stared for a long moment, then nodded and said soberly, "Right again, Spock. A Security team."

Chapter Sixteen

HOURS HAD PASSED, endless, dragging hours. The triumphant peace flight of the Klingon fleet to Earth showed no sign of starting. The Klingons on the bridge of the *Alliance* were growing visibly tenser, snapping at each other and at Kirk. "This isn't the way it was supposed to happen, is it?" Kirk said to Morith. "According to your history books, I mean?"

Morith scowled. "Obviously the history books don't tell us everything about the Tholian Incident."

"Especially that there was a standoff, with more Federation ships arriving steadily and no resolution in sight." He crossed to Morith's side. "Perhaps I could break the deadlock if I were over there, on the *Enterprise* . . ."

Morith glared at him and stalked off the command platform. Kalrind said, "Don't be too hard on him, Jim. He has something else to worry about, too—something he hasn't told you about."

"There seems to be a lot of that," Kirk said. "What, specifically?"

"There are some old documents that seem to imply that in your time the Old Klingons who controlled the Empire were trying to infiltrate your Federation."

"I encountered one of them once," Kirk said thoughtfully. "His name was . . . Darvin. That's right. We assumed he had been surgically altered to look human, but we never did figure out how he managed to *act* human. Klingons always have so much trouble behaving themselves around humans. It's their training, I suppose: they're trained to war and aggression from childhood, and they're taught to think of us as an enemy, a threat to their survival. When they *do* happen to encounter a human, they end by becoming hostile and violent, almost as if it were an instinct."

"I wish you'd put all that in the past tense," Kalrind said uncomfortably.

"It's in the present now, isn't it? Well, go on."

"We don't know much about the infiltration. The Old Klingons were so overly secretive that they apparently destroyed their own records, probably when we took control of the Empire away from them. Anyway, Morith told me that he has no way of knowing who's really in control of that Federation fleet."

"You mean he thinks it may really be Klingons?" Kirk laughed. "That's ridiculous!"

Kalrind shook her head. "No, it isn't, Jim. We think they infiltrated to very high levels. Don't you see? It would be in their own interest to abort our mission. They don't have our historical perspective on the Great Peace, of course, since it's all still in their future, but they can certainly predict from what you told your people about New Klingons that, if we succeed, everything they know will vanish. The Empire, as it became after we took control, was not a very hospitable place for them."

"I still say it's ridiculous. I spoke to Spock by subspace and to McCoy in person, and I *know* they're the men I remember."

"Of course they are," Kalrind said quickly. "I didn't mean to suggest that someone had been substituted for them. But you don't know for sure about their superiors."

Kirk chucked. "De La Jolla hasn't changed either, unfortunately."

"All I'm asking is that you put a bit more pressure on those men you *do* trust, Jim. Try to break through the stalemate."

Kirk looked at her for a long time and then finally said, "I'll try. Let's talk to Morith."

It was becoming a familiar scenario: Morith in the command chair, Kirk standing to one side, Kalrind on the other.

"Hello, Spock."

The enlarged figure on the screen at the front of the bridge nodded formally. "Captain."

"There seems to be a problem of trust, doesn't there?" Kirk clasped his hands behind him and slowly paced away from Morith, until he was standing alone on the dais. Spock's eyes followed him.

"Indeed," said the Vulcan.

"So how do we resolve this problem?" Kirk asked rhetorically. "Is McCoy there?"

"He is, Captain." The field of view widened to show McCoy standing beside the command chair.

"Bones," Kirk said, looking at the doctor, "perhaps this will help. Remember our last conversation."

As Kirk was speaking, the Klingons surrounding him were listening with interest, Kalrind most intently of all. She stepped around Morith's chair and came to Kirk's side, looking up into his face with a frown.

Kirk smiled at her and put his arm around her shoulder. He turned back to the screen and continued his conversation. "McCoy, I have *two* motes in my eye."

While the Klingons exchanged puzzled glances, McCoy took on a look of disapproval. "I can see that, Jim."

Spock, meanwhile, had bent forward and spoken in low tones into the microphone in the arm of his chair. His words were inaudible to the Klingon audience.

A sound began to form on the bridge of *Alliance*. Morith looked around, trying to locate the source of it. "What is that?"

One of the crewmen seated at a terminal below the dais yelled, "Federation transporter!" He jumped to his feet and pointed at Kirk and Kalrind. They were wrapped in a sparkling column of lights.

Morith yelled and launched himself at them . . . and stumbled through empty space and fetched up against the railing at the far end of the dais.

Kalrind looked around wildly. "Jim! Where are we?" She stiffened. "We were transported, weren't we?"

Kirk took his arm from her shoulders and stepped off the transporter platform. "Welcome aboard my favorite ship in the known universe." He nodded to the transporter technician, who grinned back at him.

"Welcome home, sir," the technician said in a scratchy voice.

"Something happen to your throat, Lieutenant?"

"It's a long story, sir."

Kirk nodded. "I'd like you to tell me about it, when all of this is over and we have the time." Kirk smiled and turned back toward the platform. Kalrind was still standing there, where they had arrived, looking confused and lost. "Jim . . .," she said, her voice trailing off.

The door slid open. Spock and McCoy entered, Security men behind them.

"Captain," Spock said in his calm, restrained way. "I'm pleased to see you."

McCoy harrumphed and pushed the Vulcan aside. "Jim!" he yelled, a deliberate contrast. He grabbed Kirk's hand and squeezed it vigorously.

Kirk grinned at the two of them. "*Plus ça change.* Bones, the mote in the eye and the beam in the eye—that's all a bit obscure, you know. I might not have caught it."

"I knew you too well for that," McCoy said triumphantly. "You're as quotation-happy as any Shakespearean actor."

"Captain," Spock cut in, "if I may recall your attention to more serious matters."

"Yes, Mr. Spock?" Kirk strove to wipe away his silly grin and look serious.

"I am happy to return command of USS *Enterprise* to you, sir."

Now the grin did go away. Kirk sighed and relaxed, a tension departing from him that he had been unaware of. He looked around the transporter room, seeing more than the walls enclosing the small space. "Yes," he said. "Yes." He shook himself and came back to the present. "I need information, Mr. Spock. Meet me in the briefing room. This way, Kalrind." Shoulders visibly stiffening, Captain James T. Kirk strode from the transporter room.

Kirk, Spock, McCoy, and Kalrind sat at a table in the briefing room, the three Federation officers at the head, Kalrind at the foot, separate from the others. Spock told Kirk what had happened after his disappearance along with the Klingon ship *Mauler:* of the storm's attack on *Enterprise,* the damage the ship had sustained, and in particular about how, when all the excitement was over, they had discovered that Uhura was unconscious.

"It was the discovery that Commander Uhura had been knocked out by a powerful electric shock, which was in turn generated by an extremely powerful signal transmitted through the transponder you had taken with you to *Mauler,* that aroused my suspicions, Captain. At first I suspected a transporter beam, although I discounted that possibility for various reasons. I then suspected that the transponder had been subjected to the Klingon cloaking device, operating at a much higher level than we have heretofore seen."

"Very strange," Kirk said. "What did you do?"

Spock glanced at Kalrind, who remained silent. He continued. "I used our copy of the Romulan cloaking device, increased its power greatly, and subjected the transponder to it. As I expected, the transponder emitted a signal of astonishing power for a fraction of a second before burning out."

Now Kirk turned and silently examined Kalrind. After a moment, he returned his attention to Spock. "Interesting, Mr. Spock. Fascinating, I might even say."

"And useful, Captain. As a result of my investigations, we now have a way to detect the use of a cloaking device from a considerable distance. Not when the cloaking device is used in a normal way, I should point out, but when its power has been increased far beyond the normal level."

"In other words," Kirk said, "when it's being used by one ship to cast a cloaking field on another."

"Precisely, Captain. Or when many ships switch on their cloaking devices simultaneously."

"Aah. Yes. Please continue."

"A few days ago, seemingly from nowhere, a large Klingon fleet suddenly appeared within the Empire, but heading toward our territory. The fleet was detected from Starbase Seventeen, which, as you know, Captain, constantly monitors Imperial space within its area of responsibility. Every Federation ship in this sector was immediately ordered to head for the point where the Klingon ships were predicted to cross the frontier. *Enterprise* was still at Starbase Seventeen for refitting, and therefore we were ordered to the frontier as well. What is significant, Captain, is that we also detected evidence of massive use of the cloaking device at the same time as the Klingon fleet appeared."

Kirk shut his eyes and sighed heavily. He looked sadly at Kalrind. "I suspected, you know, but I hoped so much that I was wrong, that you and Morith were telling me the truth."

"We were, Jim!" she insisted. "I don't understand any of this elaborate story the Vulcan has been telling you. We never lied to you!"

Kirk shook his head and stood. "Mr. Spock, get a Security detail down here. For now, I want Kalrind confined."

"Jim, no!" Kalrind rose and grasped his arm, spinning him around to face her. "You can't believe this . . ."

"I'm sorry," Kirk said, prying her fingers loose. "I really am."

The two stood silent for a moment, facing each other. Then the door to the briefing room *ssshhed* open, and two security guards entered.

"Gentlemen," Kirk said, turning his back on Kalrind. "You have your orders."

He waited till they were gone, then sank into his chair, slumping down. "She sounds as if she's telling the truth," he said plaintively.

Over his head, Spock and McCoy exchanged startled glances.

Chapter Seventeen

THE KNOCKING DRAGGED HIM from deep, tortured, unwanted sleep. With the two great fleets facing each other, shields up, and Kirk in command of the Starfleet ships, he could not afford to waste a minute. He had intended, when he lay down on his bed, only to rest, to ease the growing ache in his muscles and bones and heart. His body had betrayed him.

"Come in."

Kirk forced himself to his feet and made his way groggily to his desk. Meanwhile, the door had opened and McCoy had entered. The doctor leaned against the wall and watched Kirk stumble about his room. "You look like a prime candidate for Sickbay, Jim."

"Did you come here to make my life more miserable than it already is, Bones?"

McCoy straightened and held his hand out, palm up. "Security confiscated this from your friend." A small bottle rested in his palm. Kirk could see small red pills inside it.

"They're a medicine. I know all about them. She suffers from some kind of hereditary disease, and she has to take those once a day. Give them back to her."

"Once a day, huh?" He held the bottle up and

stared into it. "Yep. That sounds about right. Spock's told you all about Elliot Tindall, hasn't he?"

Kirk put his elbows on the desk and his face in his hands. "Bones . . ." he said. "What're you talking about?"

"Come on, Jim," McCoy said softly. "Come take a little trip with me."

"Bones, I don't have time for this."

McCoy shook his head. "This is not a joke, Jim."

Kirk looked up at him, startled by the change in tone. After a moment, he said, "Okay. Just let me soak my eyes in cold water for a few hours first."

McCoy grinned. "Don't bother. What I want to show you will open your eyes fast enough."

As they traveled toward Security, McCoy explained to Kirk who Elliot Tindall was. His story stopped at the point where Tindall attacked Spock and the Security men who had caught up with him in the transporter room.

"But where was he trying to go? And why?" Kirk asked.

"Where? The flagship of the Klingon fleet out there. Why? Because he's a Klingon."

Kirk stopped in midstride, and then started walking again. "There's more, isn't there? Go on."

"Spock was able to find a whole bunch of disguised Klingons just like Tindall, scattered throughout Starfleet and the Federation. They were all born in places that have been wiped out by one kind of disaster or another, so that there was no one who had known them in childhood. Real names, of course, so there are records of birth duplicated in central archives, but normally no actual surviving friends or relatives."

"She told me about this, you know."

"Who?"

"Kalrind."

This time it was McCoy who stopped walking for a moment. "She *did*?"

Kirk nodded. "Yes, she told me she knew of a Klingon plot to infiltrate Starfleet, but she didn't know the details. I told you these Klingons are different from the ones we're used to."

"Fascinating," McCoy said. "Well, here we are—Tindall's cell."

From McCoy's description, Kirk had expected Tindall to be an urbane, sophisticated man, a reserved European. What he saw was wild-eyed and blank-faced—and far from human.

Tindall sat on the floor at the far end of the cell, leaning back against the wall. His clothes were torn and dirty. Kirk and McCoy stood in the hallway outside the door looking in at him. Tindall's eyes roamed around the room; there was no sign of intelligence in his face. "I can't find any volunteers in Medical section to go in and take care of him," McCoy said, "and I'm not going to order anyone to do it. Security has the same problem."

While McCoy was speaking, Tindall had slowly become aware of his voice. Now his eyes focused on the two men watching him and he slowly got to his feet. He stood swaying, one hand against the wall for support, shoulders hunched. Suddenly he screamed wordlessly and leaped across the tiny cell and at the doorway.

The force field glowed with the impact, flinging Tindall back into the cell. Falling to the floor, he curled into a ball and lay shivering and moaning.

"My God, Bones, what's wrong with the man?"

"Vitamins."

"What?"

"Patience, Jim. Haven't you wondered how we knew he was a Klingon?"

Kirk raised his hands. "Blood tests, genotype. I don't know."

"Basically you're right, but the differences between us and them are more subtle than most people realize. Even normally, the differences are biochemical, not mechanical. I mean that there's nothing like the Vulcan double heart. There are the exterior differences—mainly the heavier facial bones—but that can be taken care of with surgery, and they seem to have improved their surgical abilities greatly. The biochemical differences are trickier, but the Klingons have apparently made some very major advances in biochemistry, and they now have drugs which can mask even those differences. And by the way, they also have drugs that control their moods and make it easier for them to act like gentlemen and ladies around humans."

"But you said he attacked Spock and the Security men." Kirk looked at the pitiful body huddled on the floor of the cell. Tindall was weeping quietly, steadily, hopelessly.

"And Lieutenant Crandall as well. He failed to keep taking his drug on schedule."

"A strange kind of mistake for such a successful secret agent to make!"

McCoy's forced good humor deserted him. "He was married, the poor fellow. To an Earthwoman. I should say, 'the poor woman,' shouldn't I? They seem to have been genuinely in love. Anyway, he told her some story about the drug being a supplement he had to take for his health, and she substituted something else for it before he left Earth, some pills she had that looked just like his. Vitamins."

Kirk felt sick but he had to ask the question. "What did those pills of his look like, Bones?"

Wordlessly, McCoy held up the bottle that had been taken from Kalrind.

Kirk forced himself to speak calmly. "So he didn't take them for a while, and he turned into this?"

McCoy nbodded. "After a violent stage, and then a coma. He came out of it like this. But it seems to vary. He's been an agent for a long time, which means he's been on the drug for a long time. That seems to be a factor. Klingons . . . those who've only been taking it for a short time should be okay."

"Analyze those pills."

"I don't really have to, do I?" McCoy said gently. "I can guess what they are."

Kirk snapped, "I asked for an analysis, Bones, not a guess!"

McCoy nodded and said nothing.

"I'll be on the bridge. Let me know as soon as you finish." Kirk turned to go.

"Jim. Wait a minute. Kalrind is just down the hall. She's probably confused and frightened. Just a word would help."

Kirk shook his head slowly. "No."

"Tindall isn't the only one. Thanks to Mr. Spock, we've been finding these guys all over Starfleet and the Federation government: Klingon agents, planted varying numbers of years ago, sustained by drugs so that they can act human. You have no idea what an uproar things are in back on Earth and the other major worlds. We've been hunting them down. Cloak and dagger. Exciting stuff."

"Good. Anything else?"

"Yes. I want you in Sickbay for a complete checkup. Immediately." He recognized the old look of stubbornness growing on Kirk's face, and he said, "Don't make me pull rank, Jim. As Chief Medical

Officer of the Starship USS *Enterprise*, I am formally—''

''All right!'' Kirk got his temper under control with difficulty. He knew McCoy was justified; in fact, he thought he could detect another bout of weakness approaching, like those he had suffered while with Kalrind. ''Later, I'll—No, we'll go there right now.''

''You have no doubt?''

''I have no doubt.''

''You're sure you're not detecting old injuries that have healed or been taken care of by advanced surgical techniques?''

''Jim, boy, your insides are a mess. It doesn't take a doctor of my years of experience to see that. The scanning instruments practically started screaming in revolt when I put them on you. To put it scientifically, your guts are all mangled and jangled, and it's not from the food on this ship. I won't even offer you a drink to soften the shock, because I'm afraid it would come squirting out all over your torso. Okay.'' He held up his hand. ''I'm exaggerating slightly. The fact is, your condition is consistent with your having been knocked around when *Mauler* was so shaken up. Looks to me like you had some first-aid, meatball surgery done on you by a cutter who was holding his instruments with his toes. And then they pumped you full of drugs to kill the pain and keep you pepped up.''

''Bones, I just don't understand. I felt good. I felt healed.''

''Told you about their advances in biochemistry, didn't I? They probably have the best painkillers and pepper-uppers in the known universe. Doesn't constitute a cure, though.''

He flipped through the papers on his desk, sheet

after sheet of instrument readings. "In fact, I'll go even further. Looks to me like you had a few sessions in surgery, all equally incompetent, just to keep you going and to repair the damage from the previous time. You must have been losing blood to internal bleeding. Some healing, but not enough. And by covering up the pain and giving you drug-induced energy, they encouraged you to be your normal vigorous self, which just made things worse, exacerbated the damage. It would have killed you eventually, but maybe you would have lasted long enough for their purposes.

"Someone was pumping a lot of very powerful stuff into you—so much that there's still a lot of it in your bloodstream. It won't last, though, and your condition will just keep deteriorating. So now I'm gonna put you to bed and do the job right, and you're going to have to allow a long time for recovery."

Kirk pushed himself off the examining table and onto his feet. "Sorry, Bones. I'm needed for a few hours yet. Those Klingon drugs that're still in my system will get me through, keep me alert. No arguments." McCoy started to object, but a look at Kirk's grim face silenced him.

"I'll be on the bridge," Kirk said. "I want those pills analyzed quickly. I need to know what they are."

Chapter Eighteen

KIRK IGNORED the happy smiles of greeting from the bridge crew. De Broek, the helmsman, returned to his post. Kirk resumed the command chair and sat for a long moment staring wordlessly at the static starfield displayed on the forward screen. An air of tense silence settled over the bridge as the crew perceived his mood.

Uhura broke the silence. "Captain? Morith has been requesting communication since you beamed back over."

"Well . . . " Kirk said. "He's obviously guessed where we disappeared to." He managed a weak smile at Uhura. "It's good to see you've recovered, Commander."

Uhura smiled delightedly. "And it's good to see you back where you belong, Captain. Shall I contact Morith now?"

"No, let's keep him in suspense just a little bit longer. I need to hear from Dr. McCoy before I—" As if on cue, the speaker in Kirk's chair arm buzzed, and McCoy's voice said, "Jim, I've got that analysis."

"Good work, Bones, What are you waiting for?"

McCoy muttered something to himself and then

said, "Seems my guess was a good one. Your friend had the same stuff on her that Tindall used. Mood-altering, possibly memory-suppressing."

"Memory?"

"Yes. They may not know their own backgrounds, as long as the drug is in effect. Some of those people on Earth had whole false personalities implanted in them. You have to get them off the drug for a while before the real Klingon comes back, as it did with Elliot."

"They never give up, do they?" Kirk said, thinking aloud. "As soon as we close one chink in our armor, they start probing for another." He shook himself and became aware of his surroundings, of the bridge crew staring at him with worried expressions. He forced a smile. "I don't need a mother, ladies and gentlemen. Please continue with your work." They all turned away quickly. Kirk reached for the toggle switch on the arm of his chair, missed it, frowned, tried again, missed again.

Deliberately, he put his hand down on the arm of the chair and squeezed, trying to reassert control. His entire arm was trembling and almost uncontrollable. He sat still for a few seconds, waiting for the trembling to pass. At last he was able to thumb the toggle. "Bones."

"Wondered what had happened to you, Jim. You okay?"

"Close enough," Kirk said. "I've decided what to do about Kalrind. I'm going to find out the truth. You know what I said about the New Klingons when I was still on *Alliance*. The question is this: is there such an animal, or is Kalrind able to act the way she does because of drugs?"

"Jim." McCoy's voice sounded uncertain. "Do you really need that answered anymore?"

Kirk could sense the bridge crew's gaze on him as he pondered McCoy's question. Finally, he spoke.

"As long as there's a chance, Doctor—yes, I want that question answered."

"Okay," McCoy said, sounding somewhat irritated.

"Okay. Morith said she had to take the drug every day to counteract her 'hereditary disease.' She's been without it for quite a while, now. How much leeway did the spies we caught have, before they had to take more?"

"That seems to depend on how long they've been on it. Elliott Tindall—Guess I might as well keep on calling him that! Anyway, Elliot went for a few days without another dose. Or I should say, taking what were really vitamin supplements, thinking they were his own pills. But he'd been on the drug for many years, so he'd built up an overdose in his tissues.

"How they come out of it seems correlated with how long they've been taking it, too. Elliot ended up mindless, easily angered, but also quick to drop into weeping and inactivity. When they're short-timers on the drug, they wake up fairly normal Klingons, but much angrier than usual, and therefore more dangerous. Super-Klingons, you might say. Maybe that goes away in time. We haven't been observing any of them for long enough to say.

"By the way, the *real* drug was losing its effect on Elliot even before he left Earth. His wife has told us that he was losing his normal, even-tempered disposition. He'd even moved out of the house, and he was talking about divorce. Broke her heart, poor girl. She doesn't know the rest of the story yet, either."

"We'll watch Kalrind and see what happens."

There was silence on the other end. "Could be dangerous, Jim. Elliot went through a rough few hours before he came out of it, and you saw what he came out of it as.''

''That's my decision. We'll keep her supplied with food and anything else she needs, but not those pills. Kirk out.''

He took a deep breath. ''Now, Commander Uhura,'' he said. ''Get me Morith.''

''Jim,'' Morith said, his voice at its most friendly and beguiling, ''I'm hurt that you felt the need for subterfuge.'' And indeed he did look and sound hurt.

''My ship needed me, and I needed it. I thought I had explained that to you, Morith. I suppose you would understand my feelings better if you were a military commander, rather than a civilian scientist.'' The irony sounded heavier than he had intended.

''We could have arranged something. In time.''

Kirk smiled thinly. ''In time. Yes. One hundred years, perhaps? You should have anticipated my actions. But then, none of this was in the history books, was it?''

Morith's face darkened. ''Jim, I'm very worried about the future. We discussed this, of course. This situation is endangering the Great Peace. We must ask ourselves what the consequences of our actions might be. The triumphal voyage, Jim . . . Just think of it: isn't it a beautiful picture?''

Kirk nodded. ''It is, indeed. Everything in its own time, Morith. First I have to conduct an experiment and wait for its outcome.''

Morith looked puzzled. ''I'm afraid I don't understand. Surely we can't wait for such things. This is so important! Perhaps you could beam Kalrind back here. If I could impress the importance of the situation on her, then she could come back and talk to you.''

"Sorry. She'll be participating in the experiment. Twenty-four hours should do it. I'll contact you again then."

"Surely you'll lower your shields, Kirk!" Morith said, his voice rising. "As a gesture of goodwill!"

Kirk gestured to Uhura, who cut contact with *Alliance*, leaving a momentary afterimage of Morith's surprised face on the blank screen.

Kirk stood up. He held the chair arms tightly for a moment to steady himself against a wave of dizziness. "Mr. de Broek, you have the con."

At the turbo elevator, Kirk turned and gazed at the bridge crew for a moment. "I'm proud of all of you." He entered the turbo elevator and the doors whooshed shut behind him. "Sickbay," he said. He could almost hear McCoy's voice replying, "It's about time!"

Six hours passed, a strange combination of tension and boredom, worry and weariness. On the monitor screens, Kalrind lay unchanged, sprawled on the floor in the middle of her cell, breathing shallowly. It might have been normal sleep, except that the sensors mounted in the cell told McCoy otherwise.

After four hours, watching the graphs of vital signs on his monitor, he said urgently, "We're losing her, Jim! I've got to go in there!"

"No, Bones."

McCoy looked at him, clenched his teeth, and returned to his worried vigil.

After that, the vital signs began to improve, and slowly the coma passed into natural sleep. Six hours after she had dropped to the floor unconscious, Kalrind awoke.

And she awoke and came to her feet as fast as she had fallen six hours earlier. This was not the shaken, weakened Kalrind Kirk remembered from the aftermath of her previous coma on *Alliance*. She was not the same woman in any sense. She opened her eyes and leapt to her feet simultaneously, falling into a defensive pose, but just as ready to attack as to defend. Her face wore the expression of fury just barely under control that so often characterized Klingons.

Kirk stood up. "I'm going down there." He glared at McCoy, cutting off the doctor's protest unvoiced.

As soon as Kirk was out of the room, McCoy hit the communicator. "Bridge! Mr. Spock!"

"He's in Engineering, Doctor."

McCoy cursed and tried again. "Engineering. Is Mr. Spock there."

"Here, Dr. McCoy." Maddeningly calm.

McCoy explained the situation. "He wouldn't listen to me, but he can't accuse *you* of letting emotion overrule reason. And he might need your physical strength. He's almost literally dying on his feet."

"Logically thought out, Doctor. I'm on my way. Spock out."

McCoy bit back his response; he didn't want to delay Spock at all. He watched the monitor anxiously, fearing that he would see Kirk entering Kalrind's room. The Klingon woman was now pacing around the small cell, fingers curling and opening repeatedly as if she were imagining that she was closing them around a human neck.

Kirk would have beaten Spock to the cell, rushing down a deserted hallway, but his strength gave out. He fell heavily against the wall and slid down to the floor. He struggled to rise to his feet, desperate that no crewman should come by and see him, but he couldn't do it.

He stayed where he was for a minute, trying to regain his strength. Eventually he pushed himself to his hands and knees and then, after another long rest, to his feet. He was breathing rapidly, seeing sparkling lights and dark spots in front of him. *Force of will*, he told himself desperately, and started off down the hallway again.

Spock was waiting for him outside Kalrind's cell. "Are you planning to interrogate the prisoner, Captain? A good idea."

"No, Spock, I'm planning to talk to her. Please step aside."

"Captain, you can talk to the prisoner from the hallway. The force field barrier across the doorway transmits sound quite well."

"Spock, I suppose McCoy put you up to this. Don't you know by now that that man has a mother hen somewhere in his ancestry?"

Spock's eyebrow rose. "Highly unlikely. Be that as it may, I do think his concern justified in this case. You would be in danger if you entered that cell."

"Spock!" Kirk looked up and down the hallway to make sure they were alone, and then he said, "Spock, this Klingon woman and I became very close. She's a scholar. What danger would I be in?"

Without answering, Spock stepped back and stood looking into Kalrind's cell. Kirk joined him.

The woman before them paced about her cell, walking lightly on the balls of her feet. She looked strong, alert, dangerous.

"Perhaps," Spock remarked, "the Klingons train their scholars somewhat differently from us."

This was not the woman Kirk had known. After his most recent bout of weakness, how could he argue with Spock? He stared at Kalrind, amazed at the transformation. "She doesn't seem aware of us."

"Correct, Admiral. The force field is opaque to light and sound from her side."

"Change it."

Spock hesitated, then pressed a button set into the wall beside the door. Kalrind was facing away from them and did not notice the change. Kirk called her.

She spun around, dropping into a defensive crouch. She snarled at the two figures and advanced slowly on them, hands reaching out. She touched the force field and began exploring it singlemindedly, looking for a way through it.

"Kalrind! You can't get out. Please stop before you hurt yourself."

"I'll find a way!" she growled, her voice almost a parody of the normal harsh Klingon tones. "Then I'll kill you."

Kirk glanced at Spock. The Vulcan said, "I'll be at the end of the hallway."

Kirk smiled. "Thank you, Spock." After the Science Officer had left, Kirk said to Kalrind, "You've changed."

She laughed bitterly. "You fool. Now I'm normal, not a soft 'New Klingon.' I hated being that way."

"You didn't seem to hate it. You seemed very happy."

"That drug!" she snarled. "To order a warrior to subject herself to such humiliation! When I get back to *Alliance* I'll kill Morith, too."

"That's a lot of killing for one person," Kirk said mildly. "Especially a mere scholar, an historian."

"I'm a warrior!" she shouted. "They gave me false memories, too, false feelings. I volunteered—they'll remind me of that. But they didn't warn me how much I was giving up and what kind of woman I'd become. A soft fool, just like you humans."

"Kalrind, you must have been aware of how you were acting, and yet you didn't stop yourself."

"I couldn't control it! I was trapped inside my own mind! They invented a personality and a background, and I couldn't break through the block. Only at some moments. But now that's all gone. I'm my own woman again, and I'll kill everyone responsible."

"Including me? I wasn't responsible for deceiving you. In fact, you were in love with me. That wasn't just your temporary *persona*, Kalrind: that was your true self, truly in love."

She shrieked, "With a human? The idea is disgusting, an abomination! You and all your kind are beasts; only Klingons are true people. All the other species are soft. They're inferior beings, fit only for domination, exploitation, extermination." Her voice was rising into hysteria. "We are the natural rulers of the Galaxy! When we conquer you, all of you will die. We'll kill you! I'll kill you!"

Kirk backed away, hiding from her voice, from her words.

Jekyll and Hyde, he thought. Except that in this case, the good *persona* had to fight for release and dominance, and the evil one felt trapped when that happened.

He gasped and fell full-length on the floor. As his consciousness faded, he could hear footsteps running toward him. *This can't really be happening to me*, he thought. *Right: it's all psychosomatic*. He started laughing at the idea and then faded away.

Chapter Nineteen

McCoy checked the vital-signs monitors one last time. "Amazing what it takes to get some people in to see the doctor," he said to his assistant, Joes Blankhuis. "Ready, Dr. Blankhuis?"

Joes nodded. "Any time, Doctor."

Whistling, McCoy loaded a hypospray and aimed it toward the patient's upper arm. A hand whipped up and caught McCoy's wrist.

"Bones, what're you up to?" Kirk pushed McCoy's hand away, then shoved the equipment tray aside and sat up on the operating table.

McCoy groaned. "I shoulda known it was too good to be true. Jim, you collapsed down in Security, and Spock brought you in here. You're dying, my friend. Of course, you have that choice, but I'd appreciate the chance to save you, speaking both as your doctor and your friend."

Kirk passed a hand across his forehead. "Unfortunately, I'm not up to arguing. How long do I have, then?"

"You must think I'm a Vulcan. How many decimal places do you want? No one can answer that kind of question, Jim! All I know is, you're in rotten shape and getting worse, and I'd only give you a few days. Maybe even hours."

"Good enough. The Klingon drugs are leaving me, Bones. Give me something to substitute."

"What?" McCoy yelled. "Are you crazy? I would never—"

"Bones, you know it all depends on me right now."

McCoy sneered. "The indispensable man!" *But, damn it, he really is!* "Dr. Blankhuis, you're my witness that I'm acting against my better judgment."

Joes nodded. "Agreed, Doctor. Mine, too."

McCoy glared at his assistant, then reloaded the hypospray. Kirk waited until McCoy had shot the new drug into him and he could feel its invigorating effect before remarking, "You know how much good Joes's testimony will do you if I die and you're court martialed, don't you?"

"Yeah. Combine it with a sharp stick, and it'll get me a poke in the eye."

Kirk sprang to his feet, laughing. "Good job as always, Bones. I feel great."

"Sure. And you will, too, right up until the instant you drop dead."

"And no one will even know I'm gone. When I'm on the bridge, the crew try hard not to look at me. Unwritten law of space."

"Jim, this is not a joking matter. You are literally killing yourself."

"*Salutamus,* then," Kirk said, leaving McCoy to shake his head in despair.

The strange, lightheaded mood evaporated as Kirk made his way toward the bridge, but the alertness and feeling of physical well-being remained. McCoy was right, of course; Kirk realized that. But the task circumstances had thrust upon him was more important than personal survival. That such a grim choice might become necessary was always a possibility in his profession; he had known and accepted that when he had graduated from Starfleet Academy.

Right now, he had almost sixteen hours left before Morith would be expecting him to get in contact. Morith would be getting suspicious as the hours passed and he realized what was probably happening to Kalrind.

As soon as he reached the bridge, Kirk asked for an update on the status of the deflector shields. "Still at full strength, sir," Crandall said in a sad voice.

Kirk looked at her more carefully. Aah, yes: she had tried to befriend Tindall. Well, he could sympathize with her mood. "Thank you, Mr. Crandall," he said gently. "How about the other ships in the fleet?"

Sulu answered him. "*Mary Rose* has lowered her shields, sir."

"Tell her to raise them again!" Kirk snapped. "Hold that. Uhura, pass on my urgent request to the captain of the *Mary Rose* that he put full power in his shields."

"Yes, Captain."

"Mr. Spock." Kirk didn't have to turn around to know that Spock was at his station, any more than he had checked for Uhura before giving her an order. He had registered the presence of both without conscious effort as he came onto the bridge. It was a habit of long standing, something he never thought about, but now what he had done struck him. He realized anew how much the bridge was a part of him and he of it. Once he had lost it, had been forced into a desk job. Unusual circumstances had brought him back here, to this place he loved and where he belonged. He would never give this up again. He would prefer to die here, as McCoy had warned him might happen, to drift into death in his command chair on the *Enterprise* bridge, rather than be retired and die at a desk in San Francisco. *Or develop an ulcer and die of a surfeit of milk,* he thought.

He realized Spock was speaking to him. "What, Mr. Spock?"

"You requested my attention, Captain."

"Oh, yes. Yes. Sorry. Considering what we saw in Security, Mr. Spock, it occurs to me that our prisoner may have less control over her tongue than normal."

"An interesting speculation, Captain. And a logical inference. Dr. McCoy tells me that the Klingon drug acts in part by depressing certain regulatory systems that govern physical and mental processes. As we have seen, when the drug wears off, those regulatory systems are actually even more depressed for a short time."

"I think an interrogation session might be productive."

"Indeed. Shall I ask Security to arrange one?"

Kirk shook his head. "No, Spock. I want you to conduct it. I have the feeling that your Vulcan facade will reduce her control still further."

"Perhaps so, Captain. I must point out, though, that 'facade' is not the appropriate word."

Kirk smiled. "My apologies, Spock. Give me the results in the briefing room in a couple of hours or so."

"Two hours, sir?"

"Yes, Mr. Spock," Kirk sighed. "Two hours, precisely." Sometimes he understood McCoy's short temper with the Vulcan. *I might end up in this command chair dying of an ulcer.*

As if to reinforce that fear, Uhura said, "Sir, the captain of *Mary Rose* wants to know, quote, by what authority he is interfering in the operation of my ship, end quote."

Kirk groaned. "Refer her to General Order 30, dealing with states of alert during situations where hostilities are deemed likely. . . . If she doesn't know about that, she shouldn't be in command of a starship. Don't add that part to the message!"

He could feel the ulcer beginning already.

"Your suspicions about the value of an interrogation were well founded, Captain," Spock said.

"Good. Gentlemen, let me explain." Kirk looked around the briefing room. Around the table sat Spock, McCoy, Sulu, and Scott—the inner council of officers on whose advice and support he relied so often and so heavily. Given how much he had relied on them in the past, he felt they had a right now to know more than he had yet told anyone.

First, Kirk told them about the interrogation Spock had just conducted and the reasoning that had suggested it. And then, difficult as it was for him, he told them of his experiences during the past weeks and of his travels forward and then backward in time.

"Sir," Sulu said in alarm, "we've traveled in time ourselves, but we've never had any evidence of the Klingons doing so. If they know how to do that in a controlled fashion, we're in real trouble!"

"Quite true, Mr.Sulu. But just wait. There's more to the story. I ran into inconsistencies, such as weapons on ships that were supposed to be unarmed, and New Klingons who acted just like Old Klingons under the right circumstances. So I added two and two together and got, oh, three and a half. I had been told that Old Klingons still existed in the Empire in the future and were trying to get back into power. I concluded that Morith was in league with the Old Klingons and had smuggled a bunch of them onboard his flagship, that they were planning to use the Tholian Incident somehow to regain control of the Empire. To foil that plan, I managed to beam back to *Enterprise,* along with"—he smiled slightly—"the one New Klingon I still trusted. Mr. Spock will explain to you what I should have concluded. Mr. Spock."

"Thank you, sir. I interrogated the Klingon woman, Kalrind, who is currently detained in Security Section. As the Captain hypothesized, the aftereffects of the mood-altering drug she had been taking include a lowering of normal psychological barriers. By simply questioning her and remaining unmoved by her anger, I was able to extract a good deal of interesting information from her."

McCoy snickered. "You have that effect on me, Spock, without any drugs." He looked at Kirk's face. "Sorry, Jim. Okay, Spock, go on."

"I have combined what Kalrind said to me, and earlier to the captain, with what I deduced from my own investigations of the nature of the disappearance of *Mauler* to arrive at the following," Spock said.

"There was in fact no time travel at all. Captain Kirk remained in our own time but was duped into believing he had jumped forward one hundred years. He was given a plethora of Klingon drugs to mask the symptoms of the internal injuries he sustained while aboard *Mauler,* and he has suggested himself that other drugs were included in that regimen that increased his credulousness, so that he would be more likely to believe what the Klingons told him. As we all know, Captain Kirk is not normally a particularly credulous man."

What Spock intended as a simple observation elicited grins around the table, quickly covered by hands or coughs. Kirk frowned and gestured at Spock to continue.

"My own suspicions were first aroused by what happened to Commander Uhura at the time *Mauler* disappeared. The electric shock she suffered was of mysterious origin. By experimenting with the Romulan cloaking device stored at Starfleet headquarters in San Francisco, I was able to confirm my suspicion that the shock was the result of the transponder, transmitting through Uhura's console, undergoing a cloaking field of high intensity. Nothing else was required to show me that Captain Kirk's disappearance was due to very ordinary, if daring, circumstances.

"What happened to *Mauler* was no accident. Nor was the storm that attacked the ship a natural phenomenon. It was produced by the Klingons and is indicative of their callousness toward their own people that they would so willingly risk a ship and crew."

Sulu said, "That's another dangerous capability, Mr. Spock. If the Klingons can create such a storm at will and aim it at a ship—why, that could be quite a weapon."

"Possibly, Mr. Sulu, but I doubt it. The energy expenditure must have been prodigious. Kalrind mentioned a specially built ship that was little more than a shell built around an enormous matter–antimatter reactor, the sole purpose of which was to provide the energy for the storm. While I would be interested in knowing the theory behind the storm generator, I believe it's unlikely that the Klingons would benefit from building many such ships. Still, your concern is valid; we must put the question aside for later consideration by Starfleet experts.

"Note, in fact, that the Klingons did not use the

storm as a weapon during the incident with *Mauler*. The attack by the storm on *Enterprise* was intended as a diversion and to further convince us that the storm was a natural phenomenon. But the true purpose of the entire incident was the abduction of a high-ranking Starfleet officer under such circumstances that, both to the abducted officer and to Starfleet, it would later seem plausible that he had experienced a jump in time. Our special transponder, enabling us to transport through the storm, was surely a surprise to them. I assume that the original plan was to cripple *Mauler* to the point of inoperability and 'turn off' the storm. After a rescue team had beamed aboard from whatever Federation ship had come to investigate the distress call, the storm would be 'turned on' again, along with the cloaking device, to make it seem that *Mauler* had disappeared."

He went on in a mild tone, "That they would capture someone of such a high rank and such eminence in Starfleet as Captain Kirk lay outside their plans. It is, after all, rare for a commanding officer to personally participate in dangerous missions."

"Reprimand noted, Mr. Spock," Kirk said with a hint of anger. "Please continue with the relevant facts."

"The captain has told you about the trip through the gravitational field of the supposed 'supermassive body.' However, the captain never saw any sensor readings on the body, nor did he see it directly: all he knows of it is what he saw on the *Alliance* viewscreens. I have no doubt that the image was created by means of computer graphics. That would be a trivial matter for even a Klingon ship's computers to generate. A five-year-old Vulcan child could create the necessary program in less than half an hour."

McCoy snorted and said something to Scott, who chuckled. Spock ignored them.

"That the captain experienced strange physical sensations at that moment, much like those he felt when *Mauler* disappeared, and that the Klingon fleet seemed to our sensors to spring suddenly into existence, are all explained by massive use of the cloaking device at extraordinarily high power levels."

Kirk was surprised at how disappointed he felt at Spock's mundane explanation of what had seemed at the time a magical experience. "Spock, how do you explain this: they showed me a recording of events on the *Enterprise* bridge. I saw you talking to McCoy. And a scene from Sickbay, as well. You were discussing the message I had broadcast to the fleet from *Alliance;* specifically, you were discussing my probable mental state. They claimed to be showing me recordings given them by the Federation, incomplete copies."

McCoy gave part of the answer. "We did discuss your mental state, Jim, but I don't recall ever doing that in Sickbay."

"Dr. McCoy is correct, Captain. That alone indicates that what you saw, whatever it was, was not a true recording of events in the supposed past. Was there anything specific in what you saw that would make the context unarguable?"

Kirk frowned in thought. "I'm not sure," he admitted.

"Careful suggestion in advance can cause the mind to supply missing data along the lines desired by the administrator of the experiment. The technique is common among prestidigitators."

"In other words," McCoy said, "stage magicians use misdirection, and your mind fills in the gaps in what you see the way they want you to. It was because Spock suspected all of this, Jim, that I shot a miniaturized transponder into you on the Klingon flagship."

"Yes, and it hurt, too. You could have just handed it to me, you know, and let me hold onto it."

McCoy shook his head. "Uh-uh. Scotty came up with the superminiaturized version because Spock pointed out that the Klingons probably had the one you took over to *Mauler* and would therefore recognize it. We couldn't take any chances of arousing their suspicions."

Spock added, "For that matter, that's why we decided to use the transponder, Captain. We could have found you eventually by scanning the Klingon flagship, since we knew that's where you were, but the Klingons would have detected the scan instantly and would have guessed the reason for it. They might even have chosen to kill you, rather than risk letting us get you back with whatever you might have discovered about them. We might have suspected they had done so, but we could not have proven it; we would have known only that we could not find you with our sensors."

McCoy grinned maliciously. "Also, I knew that injecting something of that size would sting like the devil. That's why I argued for its use."

Kirk shook his head. "Bones, it's a good thing you have friends in high places. But, Spock, where did they get recordings from our own ship?"

"From Elliot Tindall, or some other agent like him—someone who had attained a high enough level in Starfleet to have access to the copies of ship's recordings that are stored in San Francisco."

"Do you realize what this implies? They must have built up an enormous library, because they couldn't know who they would manage to capture, and therefore what ships he would have served on."

"Yes," Spock said. "That fact argues for extensive preparations covering every detail of the masquerade and absorbing a great deal of manpower throughout the Klingon Empire. Furthermore, their agents must have told them that we would change codes and dispositions throughout Starfleet upon the disappearance of any high-ranking officer. Thus the *Mauler* incident represented a great sacrifice of what they had managed to learn about Starfleet's current status—data that must have represented a large and long information-gathering effort. Overall, this entire episode constitutes a huge investment for the Empire—a wasted investment."

"Quite a charade," Scott said. "Elaborate. Expensive. What could the Klingons have hoped to gain from it?"

Kirk said, "Remember, Scotty, the idea was that their fleet would be escorted all the way to Earth. That was the way their invented history told the story. Once they got there, I suspect they would have launched an attack on Earth, trying to destroy the seat of Federation government and Starfleet headquarters. They even had strike craft on their ships. Maybe they planned to make a landing and capture our top people."

Scott shook his head. "Makes no sense, Captain. Our own ships would've turned on them immediately. Some of them might've escaped, but not many. There'd've been tremendous destruction on Earth, but how would that've helped them?"

"Probably more destruction to Earth than you realize, Scott," Kirk said thoughtfully. "If a few of their ships had been assigned a suicide mission and were properly equipped, and if those were the ones that started the attack, they could have destroyed much of the surface area of Earth before our defenses could have reacted. We're not equipped to handle a huge fleet that manages to get that close to one of our major worlds, you know. Starfleet plans to be able to stop them long before they get that close to our nerve centers."

"The captain is correct," Spock said. "Earth is, in effect, the capital of both the Federation and Starfleet. To the Klingon mind, its destruction would lead to the downfall of the Federation."

"Then they don't understand how our minds work, in the Federation," McCoy said. "It might work in the Empire. I mean, if someone destroyed Klinzhai, then the Empire might fall. So they just assumed that applied to us as well."

"They'll probably *never* understand how the minds of free men work, Bones," Kirk said. "It's curious that their spies could live among us for so long, drugged to behave like human beings, and yet still not come to understand the human mind. But even though they were wrong in their estimate," he pointed out, "the death and destruction on Earth would have been terrible, and certainly the Federation would have been temporarily crippled by it. In that sense, they would have achieved a large part of their planned goals.

"Well, gentlemen, I don't think we have anything more to cover. All that's left now is a final talk with Morith."

"Followed by some surgery," McCoy reminded him.

Chapter Twenty

"YOU'RE EARLY, JIM!" Morith said, his beaming face filling the front wall of the bridge. "I assume this means you've managed to smooth over all your difficulties at last and the flight to Earth can begin."

Kirk didn't bother with false joviality. "You and your fleet will retreat back across the frontier immediately, or we will open fire."

"Jim! I'm shocked! You're acting as if nothing had changed. This is a new age, Jim! We New Klingons—"

"Morith!" Kirk interrupted harshly. "We know how you generated the storm, we know about your agents in the Federation and the drugs you gave them, and we know there was no time travel and no such thing as New Klingons."

Morith's face worked for a few seconds, varying between smiling geniality and something darker and menacing. Finally he relaxed, giving up some internal struggle. "You know, Jim, the funny thing is that there really *are* New Klingons. But there never were very many of them, and we're hunting down the last of them right now. Soon the only New Klingons will be those of us with enough of the drug still in our system to act like humans!" He laughed and shook his head. "That's an irony I can still appreciate, but in a day or so my attitudes will have changed."

Kirk leaned forward. "Morith! Keep taking the drug! You can hold onto that *persona*!"

"It never was my *persona,* Jim. I wasn't altered to that extent. Not like Kalrind. I was given elements of a New Klingon, just enough so that I could do this job convincingly."

"It *was* convincing. Doesn't that mean something? Doesn't that mean that part of you is capable of friendship with humans? Someday we could still have the Great Peace!"

Morith smiled. "On your terms, not ours. Besides, didn't you hear what I just said? The few real New Klingons are being hunted down and killed. Now why would I want to put myself on that side, hmm?" He laughed again and said, "You've cost us a great deal, James Kirk. Some careers—my own included, no doubt. I won't forget what you owe us."

"My ultimatum still stands."

Morith held up his hand. "Of course. I'll give the necessary orders. Your fleet now outnumbers ours. However, I won't leave Federation space until you return Captain Kalrind."

"Immediately. Prepare your transporter room. Uhura, cut transmission." He thumbed a toggle switch on the arm of his chair. "Transporter room. Lock into the *Alliance* transporter room. One person will be beaming over in a few minutes." He thumbed the switch again. "Security. This is Captain Kirk. Deliver the Klingon woman to the transporter room. Hold her there until I arrive."

'Captain' Kalrind, eh? So much for the mild-mannered scholar. Few Klingons were so ruthless and

competent that they could climb to command rank. In the Klingon Empire, that was an accomplishment possible for only a rare and frightening type of individual.

"Yes, sir. Sir, what about Mr. Tindall? He's a Klingon, too, isn't he?"

"Mr. Tindall will be returning to Earth with us. Kirk out." *Going home*, he thought. It was Spock's idea. In the Empire, Tindall would be surplus, useless, waste material to be eliminated. Perhaps human psychologists could do something with him; perhaps someday his wife would get her husband back, after all.

Kirk rose from his seat. "Mr. Spock, you have the con."

Kirk and Kalrind stared at each other. Kirk turned to the transporter technician and said, "I'll operate the machine. You can leave."

After the tech had left the room, Kirk said to the giant in charge of the Security team, "Thank you, Corporal. You and your team may return now."

"But, Captain," the giant protested, "the prisoner disabled two of my best men! I can't leave you alone with her."

Kirk smiled. "Noted, Corporal. The prisoner is a Klingon captain. You will salute her and leave."

The Security corporal's jaw muscles bunched, but he gave Kalrind a smart salute, then one to Kirk, and he and his two subsidiary giants left the room.

"Kalrind," Kirk said quietly, "for a while, you *were* a New Klingon. What happened between us proved that friendship between our peoples *is* possible. Friendship and much more. It's up to people like us, in high positions, to make the old Organian prediction come true."

Kalrind grunted. "No real Klingon would willingly take on permanently the personality I had. You just don't understand us, Kirk. Softness repels us. We are warriors, first and foremost. We are trained to destroy the soft. You're soft, Kirk. You repel and sicken me."

She no longer spoke hysterically as she had in her cell. The violent period of overreaction to the drug had ended. But that made her words even more wounding to Kirk: now he was hearing her true feelings.

Nonetheless, he tried again. "We could build a happier galaxy, Kalrind. Peace, prosperity, cooperation—you seemed to welcome all of that before."

"That wasn't me, Kirk. That was a false personality." She stepped upon the transporter platform. "Send me back to my people immediately."

Kirk took the operator's position behind the transporter controls and fumbled with the levers. The settings were blurred. Kirk shook his head, frowned, and squeezed his eyes shut. "My feelings for you haven't changed. To me, you're the same woman you were."

Kalrind stood impassively on the transporter platform, her face wooden, as if she had not heard anything he'd said.

"Well." Kirk reached for the two levers that activated the transporter.

The settings blurred again. The levers wavered. The controls of the transporter dissolved into dancing black dots. Kirk fell against the control box and slid to the floor.

"Jim!" Kalrind gasped and leaped from the platform. She ran to the communicator panel on the wall and pressed the button. "Sickbay! Emergency in transporter room!"

She turned back to Kirk, who lay unmoving, scarcely breathing, his face white. She stood staring down at him helplessly, then dropped to her knees beside him and slid her arms under his shoulders, pulling him against her, cradling his head gently.

Her sharp hearing picked up the sound of running men. She tenderly eased Kirk back on the deck. Then she stood, pulled the two levers forward, and jumped back to the transporter platform.

Just before dematerialization began, Kalrind moved as if to go back to Kirk, but then stepped back into position and waited stoically, her gaze fixed on Kirk. When the door opened and McCoy burst into the room with Joes Blankhuis right behind him, her figure was vanishing in a sparkling column.

"You really cut it close this time, Jim. If not for my remarkable surgical skill, Starfleet would have been out one captain, and the ship's routine would have had to be disrupted for a funeral."

"I am as impressed as always by your bedside manner, Doctor."

Kirk smiled faintly at the interchange between McCoy and Spock, standing to either side of his bed in Sickbay. "If you two are trying to cheer me up," he whispered, "it's almost working."

"Maybe this'll help," McCoy said. "Near as I can figure it out, it was Kalrind who gave the alarm and summoned help when you fainted in the transporter room. Also, when you talked to her in her cell and she shrieked all of that stuff at you, my sensors showed that she was lying. Not that she wasn't really murderously angry, but the real source of her anger was horror at her own feelings. She recognized strong feelings for you in herself, and *that* frightened and repelled her."

Kirk managed to say, "Thanks for trying, Bones." *It was genuine, while we were both onboard* Alliance *and the Klingon base, I'm sure of that. Drug-induced in a way, but it must have become real.*

Those nightmares I had—real memories of emergency surgery and injections of drugs. But she asked me about "historical data," which really meant sensitive information, even though they could have got a lot of that out of me while I was under the drugs. So she must not have known what they were doing to me, all the dangerous things. She was a dupe, too.

Consoling himself with that thought, he drifted into sleep again.

On the diagnostic table beside Kirk, Elliot Tindall lay in a coma-like state again. This time his state was self-induced, not drug-induced: this time it was a flight from reality.

What had been Elliot Tindall was a mere spark, a tiny light at the center of a maelstrom of hatred and rage. Spock stood beside the tightly curled figure. His long fingers rested gently on the special contact points on Tindall's face. Their minds merged. Spock's skittered carefully about Tindall's like a starship in orbit about an incipient nova, ready to flee at the slightest hint that the explosion had begun.

Speaking to the other, mind to mind, Spock said, "Tindall. Elliot Tindall." He projected his thoughts cautiously at first. When there was no response from the roiling, red core, he tried again, louder this time: *"Elliot Tindall!"*

The reply was a mental shriek. "I AM KOL! I AM NOT ELLIOT TINDALL!"

Spock winced but held his hand in place, maintaining the channel of communication, even as the Klingon's protest echoed in his brain. "There is little future in being Kol, I think."

This time the reply was calmer and tinged with despair. "There is little future in being Elliot Tindall, either, Vulcan. There is no future for me in either place."

"Kol is disgraced," Spock suggested, "but human society does not have such rigid rules of honor and dishonor."

"I am Kol, and Kol is disgraced," the Klingon insisted. "The dishonorable rules of human society no longer matter to me."

"Tindall's work, Tindall's wife . . ." Spock thought, presenting images of Tindall's laboratory in San Francisco and of Luisa.

Tindall groaned and moved. He pushed Spock's hand away and spoke out loud, his voice rough and whispery. "I am infected by him. Tindall has made me filthy inside, but I'm still Kol, and so I will still pursue honor." He sat up and leaned back wearily against the wall.

"The honor of the warrior's code," Spock said with well-concealed irony. Humans, Klingons, Romulans—how much agony they brought upon themselves by their refusal to follow the path Vulcans chose so long ago. "The honor that demands you destroy Elliot Tindall's life and Luisa Tindall's life, even though your foolish Empire will gain nothing by the sacrifice."

"My honor will be satisfied by my self-destruction,"

Tindall insisted. "My family's honor will be saved that way."

Spock looked away, embarrassed. He found that he resented this reminder of a weakness to which even Vulcans were liable. But Tindall was lying. When Tindall had pushed Spock's hand away from his face, he had broken the mental contact, but not before Spock had seen what he had hoped to see. "You know that you are not really Kol," he said gently, "any more than you are really Tindall. You *were* Kol, but you lost that part of yourself for so many years, and you were Tindall for so many years, that you can no longer claim to be solely Klingon or human. You do not truly hate your human side. Both halves pull at you."

Tindall sighed. "True. And that's why I can't return home again."

"But which is home?" Spock persisted. *Both are home, my friend, but the choice of having both is not available to us.*

Tindall said nothing.

"Tindall was not an invader, an outsider who forced his way into your mind and possessed it for all of those years. It was a *persona* created by your psychologists and maintained with the help of drugs, but it was created out of elements of yourself. You *are* Tindall, just as you are Kol. Elliot, we can choose which part of ourselves to become, which will dominate. Klingons would reject you, but humans would not consider you tainted. To humans, it is who you are that counts, not what you are. You are an individual. You can make the life you choose for yourself."

Tindall shook his head. "Without the Klingon drugs, I would always be violent when in the company of humans."

By Vulcan standards, Spock was almost smiling. "You are doing remarkably well without drugs right now."

Tindall looked at him, startled. After a long, thoughtful pause, he said, "I was always taught that Vulcans were weaklings—a once-great warrior race that had chosen to submit itself humbly to rule by humans. There's more to it than that, isn't there?"

Spock nodded. "Much more. There always is."

When Kirk awoke again, he was alone. Was Kalrind truly lost to him forever? And if he did somehow manage to meet her again, would he be able to call up from within her the Kalrind he had grown to love? She had as much as admitted that that other woman was not a mere artifact of the drugs, that she was instead a part of Kalrind that the drugs had liberated. "Jekyll and Hyde," he muttered. "Or in this case, Hyde and Jekyll."

The picture of a future that the artificially manufactured New Klingons had painted for him was a beautiful and seductive one, one that Kirk wanted to see come about.

Jekyll and Hyde. Hyde and Jekyll. Which one was the true Klingon personality? Were both? If so, could some outside force other than drugs determine which personality dominated? In other words, he wondered, could the Federation—could James Kirk—do anything to make the New Klingon type really come about and really take over?

There was no way to know, but the possibility was a tonic.

Perhaps that future might yet exist. Perhaps there would be a Great Peace, and then even a union between the United Federation of Planets and Klingon Empire. Perhaps the peace would come about in his lifetime and it was really possible that he, James T. Kirk, would be the first Federation ambassador to the Empire.

Just possibly, Kalrind would be waiting for him.

ALL-NEW INTERVIEWS WITH
THE STARS AND CREW OF
THE ENTERTAINMENT PHENOMENON!

THE STAR TREK® INTERVIEW BOOK

BY ALAN ASHERMAN

There's never been anything quite like ***STAR TREK***. More than twenty years after Captain Kirk, Mr. Spock and the crew of the starship *Enterprise* first came to television, their original adventures continue to garner new fans—while their new movies break box-office records! Now, in dozens of interviews especially conducted for this volume, noted ***STAR TREK*** expert Allan Asherman presents an in-depth look at the people who helped create the magic of ***STAR TREK***—both on-screen and off. From Gene Roddenberry to Harve Bennett, from the man who designed the *Enterprise* to the woman who played Spock's wife, here is a wealth of never-before revealed information and fascinating trivia!

THE STAR TREK INTERVIEW BOOK

Coming in July
from Pocket Books

 123